PLATERO AND I

JUAN RAMÓN JIMÉNEZ

Platero and I

Translated by Eloïse Roach

DRAWINGS BY JO ALYS DOWNS

AUSTIN : UNIVERSITY OF TEXAS PRESS

TO THE

MEMORY OF

AGUEDILLA

THE POOR DEMENTED GIRL OF

DEL SOL STREET WHO USED TO SEND ME

MULBERRIES AND CARNATIONS

TRANSLATOR'S ACKNOWLEDGMENTS

I WISH to acknowledge gratefully the part the following persons played in the publication of this translation of *Platero and I:*

Allyn Gordon, now of Los Angeles, California, whose enthusiasm and active collaboration in the translation of the first eighteen chapters so long ago in Nacogdoches, Texas, gave the work its original impetus;

R. C. Stephenson, professor of English and of Romance languages at the University of Texas, who read the translation and gave invaluable suggestions for its final version;

Jaime Benítez, rector of the University of Puerto Rico, and Eugenio Fernández Méndez, acting director of the University of Puerto Rico Press, through whose efforts communication with Juan Ramón Jiménez was made possible;

Lewis U. Hanke, director of the Institute of Latin American Studies at the University of Texas, whose personal interviews with Dr. Benítez and others close to the author opened the way for contact between him and the University of Texas Press.

ELOÏSE ROACH

Austin, Texas
March 1, 1957

CONTENTS

PLATERO AND I

I

PLATERO

PLATERO is a small donkey, a soft, hairy donkey: so soft to the touch that he might be said to be made of cotton, with no bones. Only the jet mirrors of his eyes are hard like two black crystal scarabs.

I turn him loose, and he goes to the meadow, and, with his nose, he gently caresses the little flowers of rose and blue and gold. . . . I call him softly, "Platero?" and he comes to me at a gay little trot that is like laughter of a vague, idyllic, tinkling sound.

He eats whatever I give him. He likes mandarin oranges, amber-hued muscatel grapes, purple figs tipped with crystalline drops of honey.

He is as loving and tender as a child, but strong and sturdy as a rock. When on Sundays I ride him through the lanes in the outskirts of the town, slow-moving countrymen, dressed in their Sunday clean, watch him a while, speculatively:

"He is like steel," they say.

Steel, yes. Steel and moon silver at the same time.

3

WHITE BUTTERFLIES

NIGHT falls, hazy and purple. Vague green and mauve luminosities persist behind the tower of the church. The road ascends full of shadows, of bells, of the fragrance of grass, of songs, of weariness, of desire. Suddenly a dark man wearing a cap and carrying a pick, his face red for an instant in the light of his cigarette, comes toward us from the wretched hut that is lost in piles of coal sacks. Platero is afraid.

"Carrying anything?"

"See for yourself. . . . White butterflies."

The man wants to stick his iron pick in the little basket, and I do not prevent him. I open the knapsack, and he sees nothing in it. And the food for the soul passes, candid and free, without paying tribute to the customs.

III

TWILIGHT GAMES

AT DUSK, when, stiff with cold, Platero and I enter the purple darkness of the miserable bystreet that fronts the dry river bed, the children of the poor are playing at make-believe, frightening one another, playing beggars. One throws a sack over his head, another says he is blind, another limps. . . .

Later, with that fickleness of childhood, since they at least wear shoes and clothes, and since their mothers—though only they know how—have fed them, they become princes and princesses.

"My father has a silver clock."

"Mine has a horse."

"Mine a gun."

Clock to rouse him at daybreak; gun that cannot kill hunger; horse to take him to misery. . . .

Then the children join hands, dancing in a circle. In the darkness a little girl with fragile voice like a thread of liquid crystal in the shadow sings proudly like a princess:

"I am the young widow
Of great Count Oré. ..."

Aye, aye! Sing, dream, children of the poor! Soon, at the
awakening of your youth, spring, like a beggar disguised
as winter, will frighten you.

"Let us go, Platero."

I V

ECLIPSE

WE unwittingly put our hands in our pockets, and on our
brows we felt the fine touch of a cool shadow, as when entering a thick pine forest. The chickens began going up
their perch, one by one. All around, the countryside dark-
ened its greenness, as if the purple veil of the main altar
were spread over it. The distant sea was visible as a white
vision, and a few stars shone palely. How the whiteness of
the roofs took on a changed whiteness! Those of us who
were on the roofs called to each other more or less wittily,
small dark creatures in the confining silence of the eclipse.

We tried looking at the sun through all sorts of things:
opera glasses, telescopes, bottles, smoked glass; and from

7

all angles: the dormer window, the ladder in the yard, the granary window; through the scarlet and blue panes of the skylight. . . .

On hiding, the sun, which a moment before made everything twice, thrice, a hundred times greater and better with its complexities of light and gold, now leaves all things, without the long transition of twilight, lonely and poverty-stricken as though one had exchanged gold for silver first and then silver for copper. The town resembles a musty and valueless copper cent. How gloomy and unimportant the streets, the squares, the tower, the mountain roads.

Down in the yard Platero appears less real, different and diminished, a different donkey. . . .

V

FEAR

LARGE, round, pure, the moon comes with us. In the sleepy meadows we see shadowy forms like black goats among the blackberry bushes. At our passing, someone hides noiselessly. A huge almond tree, snowy with blooms and moonlight, its top enveloped in a white cloud, shadows the road

shot with March stars. A penetrating smell of oranges.
Dampness and silence. The witches' glen. . . .

"Platero, it is . . . cold!"

Platero—I do not know whether spurred on by his fear or
by mine—trots, enters the creek bed, steps on the moon and
breaks it into pieces. It is as if a swarm of clear crystal roses
were entangled at his feet, trying to hold him. . . .

And Platero trots uphill, shortening his croup as if
someone were after him, already sensing the soft warmth
—which seems unattainable—of the approaching town.

V I

KINDERGARTEN

IF YOU would come to kindergarten with the other children, Platero, you would learn the *ABC*'s and you would learn to write. You would know more than the donkey in the wax figures, the little mermaid's friend who appears garlanded with artificial flowers through the crystal which shows the mermaid all rosy flesh and gold in her green element. You would know more than the doctor and than the village priest, Platero.

But, although you are only four, you are so big and clumsy. In what little chair could you sit, at what table could you write, what paper and what pen would do for you, where in the chorus could you sing, say, the Credo?

No. Doña Domitila in her purple habit of the Order of the Nazarene with its yellow cord like Reyes the fisherman, would have you, at best, kneeling for two hours in a corner of the plantain garden, or she would slap your hooves with her long dry cane, or she would eat the quince meat of your lunch, or she would put a burning paper under your tail so that your ears would be as red and warm as those of the farmer's son when it is going to rain. . . .

No, Platero, no. You come with me. I will show you the flowers and the stars. And no one shall laugh at you as at a stupid child, nor shall anyone place on your head, as if you were what they call an ass, the ridiculous dunce cap with ears twice as long as yours.

VII

THE CRAZY-MAN

DRESSED in mourning, with my long brown beard and my small black hat, I must look odd riding on Platero's gray softness.

When, on my way to the vineyards, I cross the last streets, whitewashed and dazzlingly bright in the sunlight, shaggy-haired gypsy children, with sleek tanned bellies showing out of their green, red, and yellow rags, run after us shrilling a long-drawn-out call:

"Crazy-man! Crazy-man!"

Before us lies the open country. Face to face with the vast pure sky of fiery blue, my eyes—so far from my ears—open contentedly, receiving in all its quietness that nameless calm, that harmonious and divine serenity that lies in the infinitude of the horizon.

And from a distance, over the fields, sharp cries finely muffled, broken, breathless, faint:

"Crazy-man! Crazy-man!"

V I I I

JUDAS

Do NOT be frightened, old man. What is the matter? Come on, quiet down. They are only killing Judas, silly.

Yes, they are putting Judas Iscariot to death. They had one set up in Monturrio, another in Enmedio Street, another one here, in the Pozo del Concejo. I saw them last night, fixed in mid-air as if by a supernatural force, with the rope, invisible in the darkness, flung over the balcony to support them. What a jumble of old silk hats and women's sleeves, of masks of ministers and hoop skirts, under the serene stars! Dogs barked at them without quite deciding to leave, and horses, suspicious of them, were reluctant to pass under them. . . .

Now the bells are saying, Platero, that the veil of the main altar has been rent. I do not believe that a single gun in town has failed to shoot at Judas. The odor of gunpowder comes even this far. Another shot! Another!

. . . Only, today, Platero, Judas is the deputy, or the teacher, or the tax collector, or the mayor, or the midwife; and this morning before Easter, each man fires his gun under cover, against the one he hates, turned child again in a transference of vague and absurd spring make-believe.

I X

EARLY FIGS

DAYBREAK was misty and raw, a good one for early figs, and at six o'clock we set out for Rica to pick them.

Under the century-old fig trees, whose gray trunks entwined their huge muscles in the cold shadows as under a skirt, night still slept; and the wide leaves—such as Adam and Eve wore—treasured a fine web of tiny pearls of dew that whitened their new greenness. From within it and through the low emerald foliage we could see the dawn that was gradually turning to rose the colorless veils of the east.

. . . Crazy with excitement, we ran to see who would get first to each fig tree. Rociillo caught with me the first leaf of one, in a smother of laughter and swift heartbeats. "Feel here." And with her hand she took mine and placed it over her heart, above which her young breast rose and fell like a tiny imprisoned wave. Adela could hardly run, being plump and short, and she fretted from a distance. I picked a few ripe figs for Platero and put them on the seat of an old vine stump so that he would not get bored.

Adela, irritated by her own slowness, started the fig fight, with laughter in her mouth and tears in her eyes. A fig she threw at me burst on my forehead. Rociillo and I took up the fight, and much more than through our mouths, we ate figs through our eyes, noses, sleeves, necks, amid ceaseless shrill cries, which fell with the broken figs on the dawn-fresh vines. One fig struck Platero, and he became the target for the fun. Since the luckless one could neither defend himself nor reply in kind, I took his side; and a soft blue deluge crossed the pure air in all directions like rapid machine-gun fire.

A double peal of languid, tired laughter from the ground expressed the feminine surrender.

X

ANGELUS

Look, Platero, how roses are falling everywhere: blue roses, pink ones, white ones, roses with no color. One might say that the sky is dissolving in roses. See how my forehead, my shoulders, my hands, are covered with roses. . . . What shall I do with so many roses?

Do you perhaps know where all this tender flora comes from, for I myself do not know its source, which each day softens the landscape and leaves it sweetly rosy, white, and blue—more roses, more roses—like a painting by Fra Angelico, he who used to paint glory on his knees?

It might be thought that roses are being thrown down from the seven heavens of Paradise. As in a warm and vaguely colored snowfall, the roses fall on tower, on roof, on trees. Look: everything harsh turns delicate with their adornment. Roses, roses, roses. . . .

It seems, Platero, while the Angelus rings, that this life of ours loses its everyday strength and that another force within, more high-minded, more constant and pure, makes everything—as though fed from a reservoir of grace—rise

to the stars, which are already shining among the roses. . . .
More roses. . . . Your eyes, which you cannot see, Platero,
and which you raise humbly to the sky, are two beautiful
roses.

X I

THE PIT

YOU, my dear Platero, if you die before I do, are not going
to the marsh nor to the deep ravine-like pit beside the
mountain road in the old town crier's cart like poor donkeys and dogs and horses whom no one loves. You will not
be, with your fleshless ribs bloody from the crow's picking
—like the bare ribs of a boat against the scarlet sunset—

an ugly spectacle for the travelers to San Juan Station in the six o'clock coach; nor lie swollen and rigid on the rotten shells of the pit to frighten thrill-seeking children on their Sunday evening walk through the pine grove when they gaze in fear and curiosity over the edge.

Do not worry, Platero. Live in peace. I shall bury you at the foot of the tall round pine in the orchard which you like so well. You shall lie beside gay and beautiful life. The children will play around you, and the young girls will learn to sew sitting in low chairs by your side. You will know the verses brought to me by solitude. You will hear the singing of the washer girls in the orange grove, and the noise of the well will add joy and coolness to your sleep. All the year round, the larks, the titmice, and the young green finches will form above you, in the perennial verdure of the pine top, a brief canopy of music between your quiet slumber and the blue of the infinite sky.

X I I

THE THORN

ON ENTERING the pasture lands Platero begins limping. I jump quickly to the ground.

"What is the matter, child?"

Platero lets his right forefoot hang limp without weight or strength, barely touching the burning sand of the road, showing the frog of the hoof.

With greater solicitude, no doubt, than that shown him by old Darbón, his doctor, I stoop to examine the bruised foot. A long green orange-tree thorn is stuck in it like a little round emerald dagger. All sympathy with Platero's pain, I pull out the thorn and take the poor fellow to the brook of the yellow lilies so that the running water may lave the little wound with its long pure tongue.

Then we go on toward the white sea, I leading, he following, still limping, his head knocking softly against my body at each faltering step.

XIII

THE SWALLOWS

THERE she is, Platero, black and sprightly in her gray nest on the frame that holds the image of the Virgin of Montemayor, a nest that has always been unmolested. The luckless bird is bewildered. It seems to me that this time the poor swallows made a mistake, as the chickens did last week in going to roost at two o'clock during an eclipse. Spring had the coquetry to arrive early this year, but she has been obliged to take her tender nakedness, all ashiver, back to the cloudy bed of March. It is sad to see the virgin blossoms of the orange grove die in the bud.

The swallows are back, Platero, and yet one can hardly hear them, as in other years, when on their first day back they would greet everything and curiously examine it, chattering tirelessly in their fluty chirping. They would tell the flowers all they had seen in Africa, about their two trips across the sea, how they sometimes lay on the water with one wing as a sail, or on the masts of ships; they would talk of other sunsets, other dawns, other starry nights. . . .

They do not know what to do. They fly about, mute, bewildered, as ants walk when some child stamps out their trail with his feet. They dare not go up and come down Nueva Street in insistent straight line with the little flourish at the end, nor go down to their nests in the wells, nor perch, in classic post-card fashion, by the white transformer on the telegraph wires, through which the wind hums. . . . They will freeze to death, Platero!

X I V

THE STABLE

WHEN I go to see Platero at noon, a transparent ray of the midday sun is kindling a great patch of gold on the soft silver of his back. Beneath his body, on the dark ground, which is vaguely green and tinges everything with emerald, the old roof rains clear coins of fire.

Diana, who has been playing between Platero's legs, comes dancing toward me and puts her forepaws on my chest, eager to lick my mouth with her pink tongue. Perched on the highest part of the manger, the goat regards me with curiosity, moving her delicate head from side to side with feminine distinction. In the meantime, Platero, who had already greeted me with uplifted voice before I entered, tries to break free from his rope, bringing all his gay sturdiness into play.

The skylight lets in the iridescent treasure of the zenith, and through it I climb for a moment up a sunbeam to the sky, away from these friends. Presently, back on earth, I step on a rock and look out upon the fields.

The green landscape is swimming in the fragrant and

drowsy flood of noonlight, and against the clear blue framed by the grimy walls breaks the sweet ringing of a bell.

X V

THE CASTRATED COLT

HE WAS black, with scarlet, green, and blue iridescence, all silvery like beetles and crows. In his young eyes there flashed at times a living fire, like the one on the clay pot of Ramona, the chestnut-roaster of Marqués Square. What a smart tinkling of hoofbeats as he trotted into town from the sandy Friseta, the champion, along the cobblestones of

Nueva Street. How light, how nervous, how sharp he was, with his small head and slender legs.

In his noble fashion, with free and prideful gait, in playful mood, he passed through the low door of the big barn, blacker than himself against the red sun of the castle, which stood as dazzling background for the aisle. Then, stepping over the pine log that served as door lintel, he filled the green barnyard with gladness and with the din of chickens, pigeons, and sparrows. Four men awaited him there, with hairy arms crossed above colorful shirts. They led him under the pepper tree. After a brief, rough struggle, first affectionate, then blind, they threw him down on the barnyard dung, and, while they sat on him, Darbón, the veterinarian, performed his surgery, putting an end to the colt's mournful and magical beauty.

"Thy unus'd beauty must be tomb'd with thee,
Which used, lives th'executor to be,"

says Shakespeare to his friend.

The colt, become horse, was left docile, covered with sweat, exhausted, and sad. It took only one man to draw him up, cover him with a blanket, and lead him away slowly down the street.

Poor useless cloud, lightning flash yesterday, tempered and solid. He was now like an unbound book. It was as though he was no longer on the earth, as though between his shoes and the stones a new element isolated him, leaving him without awareness, like an uprooted tree, like a memory, in the violent, whole, round morning of spring.

24

X V I

THE HOUSE ACROSS THE STREET

IN MY childhood, Platero, the house across the street always
held great enchantment for me. First, on Ribera Street, the
little house of Arreburra, the water-vendor, with its yard
to the south, always golden in the sun, from which I could
see Huelva by climbing the garden wall. Once in a while I
was allowed to go there for a moment, and Arreburra's
daughter, who then seemed to me a woman grown and now
that she is married seems to me as then, would give me
sweet quinces and kisses. . . . Later, on Nueva Street—and
then Cánovas, then Fray Juan Pérez—the house of Don
José, the confectioner of Seville, who dazzled me with his
yellow kid boots, who used to hang eggshells on the century
plant in his courtyard, who used to paint his doorway canary
yellow with aquamarine stripes, who used to come, at times,
to my house, where my father would give him money, and
he would talk to my father of the olive grove. . . . How
many of my childhood dreams have been rocked by the old
myrtle tree, which I could see from my balcony, covered
with sparrows, above Don José's roof. There were, to me,

25

two myrtle trees, which I never saw as one: one that I could see from my balcony, top rife with wind or sun; the other, the one that I saw in Don José's yard, from the trunk up. . . .

On clear evenings, on rainy noondays, at the slightest change of every day or every hour, what an interest, what an extraordinary attraction it had for me, that house across the way that I saw from my grating, from my window, from my balcony, in the silence of the street.

XVII

THE LITTLE IDIOT

EVERY time we returned by San José Street the little idiot would be sitting at the door of his house, watching people pass. He was one of those wretched children to whom the power of speech and the gift of beauty never come; gay in himself, sad to look upon; all in all to his mother, nothing to others.

One day, after the evil black wind had passed by the white street, the child was no longer at his door. A bird was singing in the deserted threshold, and I was reminded of Curros, more the father than the poet, who sought in vain

for the spirit of his lost child among the yellow-winged
Galician butterflies:

> "Volvoreta d'aliñas douradas . . ."
> ("Butterfly of the golden winglets . . .")

Now that spring has come, I think of the little idiot who
went to heaven from San José Street. He must be sitting in
his little chair beside the roses watching with reopened
eyes the golden passing of the blest.

XVIII

THE GHOST

THE greatest fun for Anilla the butter-maker, whose impetuous and fresh youth was an endless fountain of gaiety,
was dressing up as a ghost. She would wrap herself in a
sheet, add flour to the lily whiteness of her face, put garlic
cloves on her teeth, and when, after supper, we half-dozed
in the little living room, she would suddenly appear from
the marble staircase, carrying a lighted lantern, walking
slowly, mute and imposing. Dressed thus, it was as if her
nakedness had become a robe. Yes. The sepulchral vision
that she brought from the dark heights caused terror, but at
the same time her whiteness alone fascinated with some
vague sensual fullness. . . .

I shall never forget, Platero, that September night. For an
hour the storm had been beating over the town like a sick
heart, discharging water and hail to the despairing insistence of lightning and thunder. The cistern was overflowing
and had flooded the courtyard. The final accompaniments
—the nine-o'clock coach, the vesper bells, the postman—
were over. . . . Shaking with fear, I had gone to the dining
room for a drink, and in the green whiteness of a lightning

flash, I saw the Velardes' eucalyptus tree—the cuckoo tree, as we called it, which fell that night—doubled over the roof of the tool shed. . . .

Suddenly a frightful dry noise, like the shadow of a cry of light that blinded us, shook the house. When we came back to reality, we were all in a different spot from the one we had occupied a moment before, and each one as though alone, without anxiety or concern for the others. One complained of a headache, another of smarting eyes, another of his heart. . . . One by one we returned to our places.

The storm was abating. . . . The moon, between enormous clouds that split from top to bottom, lit with her white fire the water that overflooded the courtyard. We walked about looking at everything. Lord kept running to the yard steps and away again, barking crazily. We followed him. . . . Platero, near the night-blooming vine whose wet flowers exhaled a nauseating odor, lay Anilla, dead, dressed as a ghost, the lantern still burning in her lightning-blackened hand.

X I X

LANDSCAPE IN SCARLET

THE hilltop. The setting sun lies pierced by his own crystal spears, bleeding purple and crimson from every vein. Before his splendor the green pine grove is dulled, turns vaguely red; and from the flushed transparent grass and small flowers a penetrating and luminous essence emanates.

I stop entranced in the twilight. Platero, his black eyes turned to scarlet by the sunset, walks softly to a pool of crimson, violet, rose-colored waters; gently he sinks his mouth in these mirrors, which again become liquid at his touch; and there is a profuse passing of dark waters up his huge throat.

I know this place well; but the moment has changed it and made it portentous. At any moment an unearthly adventure may befall us, an abandoned castle may loom before us. . . . Evening prolongs itself beyond itself, and the hour, imbued with the spirit of eternity, is infinite, peaceful, beyond sounding.

"Come, Platero."

X X

THE PARROT

WE WERE playing with Platero and the parrot in the garden of my friend the French doctor when a young woman,
disheveled and anxious, came downhill toward us. Before
reaching us she turned her anguished black eyes toward me
and pleaded:

"Young master, is the doctor there?"

Behind her came a number of dirty, ragged children who
panted and kept looking up the road; last of all came
several men carrying another man, livid and exhausted. He
was a poacher, one of those who hunt deer in the Doñana
preserve. His gun, an absurd old thing tied together with
woven bark, had misfired, and the hunter had the bullet
in his arm.

My friend approached the wounded man with friendli-
ness, removed the dirty cloths from the wound, washed off

the blood, and began feeling the bones and muscles with his fingers. From time to time he would say to me:

"Ce n'est rien. . . ."

Dusk was falling. From Huelva came an odor of marsh, of resin, of fish. . . . Against the rosy sunset the orange trees showed their rounded thick emerald velvet. In a lilac bush, lavender and green, the parrot, green and red, came and went, examining us with his little round eyes.

The poor hunter's tears were filled with sunlight; at times he uttered a muffled cry. And the parrot would say:

"Ce n'est rien. . . ."

My friend was dressing the wound with cotton and bandages.

The poor man:

"Ooooh!"

And the parrot among the lilacs:

"Ce n'est rien. . . . Ce n'est rien. . . ."

XXI

THE ROOF

You, Platero, have never climbed to the flat roof of the house. You cannot know how one's heart expands with the

32

joy of breathing, when, attaining it from the dark and narrow wooden stairway, one feels the heat of the full daytime sun and knows himself flooded with blue, as though
touching the sky itself, blinded by the whiteness of the lime
with which, as you know, the brick floor is covered, so that
the water from the clouds may reach the cistern clear and
clean.

What enchantment on the roof! The bells of the tower
ring within you, on a level with your heart, which beats
faster; you can see in the distant vineyards the hoes gleaming with a glint of silver and sunlight; you dominate everything: other roofs; yards where forgotten people work,
each at his own task—the chairmender, the painter, the
hooper—spots that are trees in barnyards, with the bull or
the goat; the cemetery to which there comes from time to
time, small and black and unnoticed, a humble third-class
funeral; windows at which a girl in a white bodice careless-
ly combs her hair and sings; the river, and a boat that never
quite reaches port; granaries where a lone musician prac-
tices on his horn—or where blind, violent love is having its
way. . . .

The house has disappeared like an underground cellar.
How strange, through the crystal skylight, ordinary life below: words, sounds, even the garden, so beautiful in itself;
you, Platero, drinking at the trough, not seeing me, or playing like a simpleton with the sparrow or with the turtle.

XXII

RETURN

PLATERO and I were returning from the mountains heavily loaded: he with sandalwood, I with yellow lilies.

It was April dusk. Everything that in the west had been limpid gold was now limpid silver, a smooth luminosity of Cape jessamine petals. Then the vast sky became transparent sapphire; then emerald. Sadness held me like a shroud. . . .

From the hilltop the one tower of the town, the church steeple crowned with blue tiles, acquired in the clarity of the hour a monumental aspect. For the moment it was the Giralda from a distance. . . . And my yearning for Seville, acute in springtime, found in the sight a melancholy comfort.

Return. . . . Where? From what? To what? For what? But the lilies I carried were more odorous in the warm freshness of approaching night; their fragrance was more penetrating and at the same time more vague, coming from the unseen blossoms, as if they had become all odor, intoxicating the body and the soul in the solitary darkness.

"Oh, soul of mine, lily in the shadow," I said. And suddenly I remembered Platero, whom, though on him, I had forgotten, as if he were part of my body.

XXIII

THE LOCKED GATE

WHENEVER we went to the Diezmo store, I would always return along the wall on San Antonio Street and stop at the locked grilled gate leading to the open country. I would place my face against the bars and look to the right and to the left, straining my eyes eagerly as far as my sight could reach. From its very threshold, worn and lost in the nettles and mallows, a path starts and disappears, downgrade, at Angustias. And below its hedge there is a wide, low road that I have never traveled. . . .

What a magical fascination it was to see, through the iron squares of the gate, the selfsame landscape and sky outside it. It was as though a roof and wall of illusion separated this particular view from the rest, to leave it alone behind the closed grille. And I could see the highway, with its bridge and its smoke poplars, and the brick kiln, and the Palos hills, and the steamers of Huelva, and, at nightfall, the lights of Riotinto wharf, and the tall and lonely eucalyptus tree of Arroyos against the purple of the fading sunset. . . .

The storekeepers used to tell me, laughing, that the gate was not locked. . . . In my dreams, with the transmutations of unchanneled thought, the gate opened into the most prodigious gardens, into the most marvelous fields. . . . And just as one time, trusting a nightmare I had had, I tried to fly down the marble stairway, time and again I went of a morning to the gate, convinced that I would find behind it what my imagination added—I do not know whether consciously or unconsciously—to reality. . . .

XXIV

DON JOSÉ, THE CURATE

Now, Platero, he goes forth, very holy and full of honeyed words. But the one that in reality is always angelic is his she-ass; she is a lady.

I think you saw him in his orchard one day, wearing sailor's breeches and broad-brimmed hat, throwing curses and rocks at the urchins that were stealing his oranges. A thousand times on Fridays you have seen poor Baltasar, his houseboy, dragging his rupture, which looks like a circus balloon, along the roads, coming to town to sell his miserable brooms or to pray with the poor for the dead relatives of the rich. . . .

Never have I heard a man utter worse profanity nor raise higher heaven with his oaths. It is true that he no doubt knows—at least, so he says in his five o'clock mass—where and how things are up there. . . . The tree, the clod, the water, the wind, the chestnut bloom—all this, so graceful, so fresh, so pure, so bright, seems to be for him an example of disorder, hardness, coldness, violence, ruin. By the end of each day the rocks in his orchard lie in a differ-

ent place, having been hurled in furious hostility against birds and washerwomen, children and flowers.

At vespers everything changes. Don José's silence is heard in the silence of the countryside. He dons his habit, cloak, and low-crown hat, and, almost without seeing, enters the dark town on his slow she-ass, like a carnival image on a skeleton. . . .

X X V

SPRING

"O what sparkles and odors!
O how pasture grounds rejoice!
O what joy and mirth are heard!"
—*Popular ballad*

MY morning nap is disturbed by a devilish noise of children and I am in an ill-humor. No longer able to sleep, I leave my bed in despair. Then, looking out from my open window, I realize that it is the birds whose shrill clatter has disturbed my slumbers.

I go down to the garden and sing thanks to the God of the blue day. Free concert of singing bills, fresh and endless

music. The swallow, fanciful one, utters her warbling from the well; the blackbird whistles on the fallen orange; the fiery golden oriole chatters from evergreen to evergreen; the blue titmouse laughs long and daintily on the top of the eucalyptus tree; and in the tallest pine the sparrows argue outrageously.

What a morning! The sun spreads his gold and silver gladness on the earth; myriad-colored butterflies flit everywhere, among the flowers, through the house—now in, now out—above the spring. Everywhere the countryside bursts open to a bubbling of new and wholesome life.

It is as though we were inside a great honeycomb of light, which might be the heart of an immense, calid, scarlet rose.

X X V I

THE CISTERN

LOOK at it: the last spring rains have filled it to the brim, Platero. It has no echo now, nor can one see, in its new depth, the reflection of the oriel window bathed in sunlight, prismatic jewel above the yellow and blue pattern of the glass patio roof.

You have never been down in the cistern, Platero. I have; I went down when it was emptied, many years ago. Listen; it has a long underground gallery, and then a very small room. When I entered it, the candle I carried was snuffed out by the fingers of the darkness, and a salamander crawled over my hand. Two icy sensations crossed each other in my breast like two swords, or like the crossbones under a skull. The whole town is honeycombed with cisterns and galleries, Platero. The largest cistern is the one in the courtyard of the ancient citadel of the castle. The best one is this one at my house, which, as you see, has the curbstone carved in one piece of alabastrine marble. The gallery of the church goes as far as the Puntales vineyard, and there it opens on the fields, near the river. The one that starts at the hospital no one has ever dared to follow to its end, because it never ends.

I remember how when I was a child the sobbing murmur of the rain that fell from the flat tiled roof into the cistern troubled my sleepless hours. Then, in the morning, mad with eagerness, we would go to the cistern to see how high the water had reached. When it was up to the rim, as now, what surprise, what excitement, what exclamations. . . .

Well, Platero, now I am going to give you a bucketful of this pure fresh water, from the same bucket that old Villegas used to drink from, poor Villegas, whose body was already dried up with cognac and brandy. . . .

X X V I I

THE MANGY DOG

HE USED to come sometimes, lean and panting, to the garden house. The poor thing was always running from someone, accustomed to shouts and stones. Even other dogs snarled at him. And he would go back in the noonday sun, slow and sad, down the hill.

That afternoon he had followed Diana. As I was coming out, the keeper, who on an evil impulse had aimed his gun, fired at him. I had no time to stop him. The wretched dog, with the bullet in his body, whirled dizzily for a moment with a round sharp howl, and fell dead under an acacia bush.

Platero, head erect, kept his eyes fixed on the dog. Diana was frightened and kept trying to hide behind one or the other of us. The keeper, perhaps in remorse, repeated long explanations to no one in particular, angry and helpless in this effort to silence his conscience. A veil hid the sun, as in mourning, a large veil, like the tiny one that clouded the one good eye of the murdered dog.

Beaten to exhaustion by the sea wind, the eucalyptus wept ever more loudly toward the storm in the deep crushing silence that noon spread above the dead dog throughout the yet golden countryside.

XXVIII

THE POOL

WAIT, Platero. Or browse a while in this tender meadow, if you prefer. But let me look at this beautiful pool, which I have not seen in years.

Look how the sun, piercing its turbid waters, lights up the deep green-gold beauty which the heavenly cool lilies on the margin contemplate enraptured. The light forms velvet-soft ladders descending in repeated labyrinth; magical grottoes with all the ideal aspects that a dream mythology might bring to the exuberant imagination of a brooding painter; graceful gardens that the tender melancholy of a mad green-eyed queen might have created; palaces in ruins like the one we saw in the twilight sea when the setting sun fell obliquely on the silent waters. . . . And more, and more, and more: all that the strangest dream might gain, drawing fugitive beauty by her infinite robe, from the remembered hour of a pain-filled spring in a garden of forgetfulness, that had never quite been. . . . Everything in miniature, yet immense, because distant; key to innumerable sensations, treasure house of the most ancient magician of fevered dreams.

The pool, Platero, used to be my heart. Thus did I feel it in me, beautifully poisoned in its solitude with prodigious repressed extravagances. When human love wounded it, opening its dam, the poisoned blood flowed out of it, leaving it pure, clean, and gentle, like the Llanos brook, Platero, in the most open, most golden hour of April.

Sometimes, nevertheless, a pale ancient hand brings it back to its former green and lonely pool and leaves it there enchanted, outside itself, responding to the clear summons, "to sweeten its grief," like Hylas to Alcides in Chénier's idyl, which I have read to you, Platero, with a voice "unknowing and vain."

XXIX

APRIL IDYL

THE children took Platero with them to the brook of the poplars, and now they are bringing him back trotting, in the midst of pointless playing and senseless laughter, loaded with yellow flowers. It rained on them down there—that fleeting cloud which veiled the green meadow with its threads of gold and silver on which there trembled, like a lyre of tears, the rainbow. And in the drenched hair of the little donkey the wet bellflowers are still dripping.

46

Fresh, gay, sentimental idyl! Even Platero's braying
sounds tender under the sweet, rain-drenched load. From
time to time, he turns his head and bites off the flowers his
big mouth can reach. The white and yellow blooms hang
for a moment from his mouth, streaked with his greenish
slaver, then disappear into his round, cinched belly. If one
could only eat flowers like you, Platero, and not suffer.

Ambiguous April evening! The brilliant eyes of Platero
reflect the hour of sun, against whose setting above the
field of San Juan is seen another rosy raveled cloud raining.

X X X

THE CANARY'S FLIGHT

ONE day the green canary—I do not know how or why—
flew out of his cage. He was an old bird, a sad legacy from
a dead woman, which I had not set at liberty for fear that he
might starve or freeze to death, or that he might be eaten
by the cats.

All morning long he flew about the pomegranate blossoms in the garden, through the pine tree by the gate,
among the lilacs. And all morning long the children sat on
the porch, absorbed in the brief flights of the yellowish
bird. Platero rested close to the rosebushes, playing with a
butterfly.

In the late afternoon the canary came to the roof of the
large house, and there he remained a long time, fluttering in
the soft light of the setting sun. Of a sudden, without anyone's knowing how or why, he appeared in his cage, gay
once more.

What a stir in the garden! The children leaped about,
clapping their hands, rosy and laughing as the dawn; Diana, mad with joy, followed them, barking at her own

tinkling bell; having caught their mirth, Platero capered around like a wild young goat, stood on his hind legs dancing a rude waltz, and then, standing on his forefeet, kicked his hind feet in the clear warm air. . . .

XXXI

THE DEVIL

OF A sudden at a hard and single trot, the donkey, looking twice as dirty in the tall dust cloud, appears by Trasmuro corner. A moment later, breathless and holding on to their ragged breeches, which leave their dark bellies exposed, urchins appear, throwing vine props and rocks at him.

He is black, huge, old, bony—like a certain archpriest—
so bony indeed that he looks as though his bones will come
through anywhere in his hairless hide. He stops, and, showing yellow teeth like large horse beans, he brays fiercely
skyward with an energy that belies his ungainly old age. . . .
Is he a strayed donkey? Do you know him, Platero? What
do you suppose he wants? From whom must he be fleeing
at that ungainly, violent trot?

On seeing him, Platero first pricks up both ears to a single
point, then he lowers one, leaving the other standing, and
comes to me, tries to hide in the ditch and to run away at
the same time. The black donkey passes beside him, rubs
against him, pushes on his saddle, sniffs him, brays by the
convent wall, and trots away, down Trasmuro.

There is in the heat a strange moment of chill—mine?
Platero's?—in which things are topsy-turvy, as if the lower
shadow of a black cloth before the sun had suddenly hidden the dazzling solitude of the bed of the alley, where the
abruptly still air asphyxiates. Gradually the distant recalls
us to the near. Above us there is the changing sound of
many different voices from Pescado Plaza, where fishmon-
gers just arrived from Ribera are singing the praises of their
wares: flounder, surmullets, dace, pintano, spider crabs;
the pealing bell announcing tomorrow's sermon; the scis-
sors-grinder's whistle.

Intimidated, Platero still shivers now and then, his fear-
filled eyes searching mine in the mute stillness into which
we have both fallen without quite knowing why. . . .

"Platero, I believe that that donkey is not a donkey. . . ."

And Platero, silent, shivers again all over with one single shiver, softly noisy, and keeping his distance turns a low and sullen glance toward the ditch. . . .

X X X I I

LIBERTY

MY ATTENTION, lost in the flowers that lined the path, was recalled by a little bird bath'ed in light, which unceasingly fluttered his wings in the wet green mead. We approached slowly, I in front, Platero behind me. There was nearby a shadow-dark watering place, and some treacherous boys had set a snare for birds. The sad little captive would rise as far as he could, calling unconsciously to his sky brothers.

The morning was clear, pure, transpierced with blue. From the nearby pine grove there fell a light concert of excited trills that swelled and softened without fading in the gentle golden sea wind that rocked the treetops. Poor innocent concert, so close to the evil heart.

I got on Platero and, urging him with my legs, climbed up to the pine grove at a sharp trot. Arriving under the somber leafy canopy, I clapped my hands, sang, shouted. Platero, entering into the spirit of my effort, brayed harshly once and again. And the deep sonorous echoes responded as from the depths of a deep well. The birds fled singing to another grove.

Platero, in the midst of the distant maledictions of the angry urchins, rubbed his hairy head against my heart, thanking me to the point of hurting my chest.

XXXIII

THE ROMANIES

LOOK at them, Platero, stretched out full length on the sunny sidewalk, as tired dogs stretch out their very tails.

The young woman, a statue of dirt, her abundant copper-colored nakedness overflowing inside her rags of scarlet and green wool, is pulling up the long dry grass that her hands, black like the bottom of an iron kettle, can reach. The little girl, all hair, is drawing charcoal obscenities on the wall. The little boy is wetting over himself like a fountain in its cup, crying for fun. The man, the monkey, scratch themselves, the former his mat of hair as he mutters, the latter his ribs, as if he were playing a guitar.

From time to time the man sits up, then rises, goes to the middle of the street, and·with indolent force beats the drum and looks up at a balcony. The girl, while the child kicks her, sings, swearing unashamedly, in tuneless monotony. And the monkey, whose chain weighs more than he does, missing his cue, for no reason rings the bell and then begins to search among the pebbles in the ditch, as if to find a soft one.

Three o'clock. . . . The station coach leaves, up Nueva Street. The sun, alone.

There you have, Platero, Amaro's family ideal. . . . A man like an oak, scratching himself; a woman, like a vine, stretched out; two children, a male and a female, to propagate the race; and a monkey, small and weak like the world, who earns a living for all of them, picking his fleas. . . .

XXXIV

THE SWEETHEART

THE clear sea breeze comes up the red slope, reaches the meadow of the hilltop, laughs among the delicate little white flowers; later it becomes entangled in the young fir trees and rocks the glowing rose and golden cloudlets, swelling them like subtile sails. The entire evening is now a sea wind. And sun and wind give a restful well-being to the heart.

Platero, happy, agile, well-disposed, is carrying me. It is as if I did not weigh on him. We go uphill as easily as we go downhill. In the distance, a brilliant colorless ribbon of sea oscillates between the last pine trees in a seeming island landscape. In the green meadow far below, the white-footed donkeys leap from shrub to shrub.

A sensuous tremor pervades the glades. Of a sudden, Platero pricks up his ears, dilates his nostrils in his upraised head until they almost reach his eyes, and exposes his large yellow teeth. He is breathing in from the four winds some deep, indefinable essence that must fill his heart with anguish. Yes. There, on another hill, fine and gray against the

55

blue sky, is his beloved. And double brayings, long and sonorous, break with their clamor the luminous hour, then fall like twin waterfalls.

I have had to oppose the loving instincts of my poor Platero. The fair beloved watches him pass, as sad as he, with her jet-black eyes full of reproaches. . . . Vain, mysterious call, rolling over the white daisies, like an instinct made flesh.

And Platero trots unwillingly, trying at every moment to turn back, a reproach in his little restrained trotting:

"It is hard to believe, it is hard to believe, it is hard to believe. . . ."

X X X V

THE LEECH

JUST a moment. What is it, Platero? What is the matter?"

Platero's mouth is bleeding. He coughs, and he walks more and more slowly. I understand in a moment. On passing by Pinetree Fountain this morning, Platero drank. And though he always drinks in the clearest spot and through tight-clenched teeth, a leech must have fastened itself on his tongue or on the roof of his mouth.

57

"Wait, old man. Show me."

I ask Raposo, the farmer who has come down from the almond grove, for help, and between us we try to open Platero's mouth. He has closed it fast, as with Roman concrete. I realize sorrowfully that poor Platero is less intelligent than I had thought. Raposo takes a stout stick, breaks it in four pieces, and tries to insert a piece between Platero's jaws. It is not an easy undertaking. Platero raises his head to the zenith, standing on his hind legs; he flees, he runs hither and yon. Finally, in an unguarded moment, the stick goes into Platero's mouth. Raposo mounts the donkey and pulls back on the stick, holding the ends of it with both hands so that Platero will not drop it.

Yes, far inside, full and black, the leech is fastened. I pull it off, using two twigs as pincers. It looks like a little sac of red ocher or a tiny wineskin filled with red wine; and against the sunlight it is like the comb of a turkey angered by a red rag. So that it may never again suck the blood of a donkey, I slit its body and cast it into the brook, where for a moment Platero's blood gives a red tinge to the foam of a brief whirlpool.

THE THREE OLD WOMEN

GET up here, Platero. We must let those poor old women
pass. . . .

They must be coming from the beach, or from the hills.
Look. One is blind, and the other two lead her. They are

probably coming to see Dr. Luis, or to the hospital. See how very slowly they walk, with what care, with what seriousness the two who can see act. They look as if all three were afraid of meeting death itself on the road. Do you see how they extend their hands gropingly before them, as if to ward off the very air, thrusting aside imaginary dangers? Do you see how, with absurd tenderness, they push back even the lightest flowering branches, Platero?

You will fall, little one, if you are not careful. . . . There. Listen to their plaintive words. They are gypsies. Look at their picturesque dresses, patched and beruffled. See? They wear no shawl; their erect carriage has not suffered with age. Blackened, perspiring, dirty as they are, blurred in the luster of the hot midday dust, there is yet apparent in them a lean, rude beauty, a dry and harsh reminder.

Look at the three of them, Platero. With what confidence they bring age to life, permeated by this spring that causes the thistle to bloom in yellow under the vibrant sweetness of its fiery sun.

X X X V I I

THE CART

In the big creek, which the rains had swelled as far as the vineyard, we found an old cart stuck in the mud, lost to view under its load of grass and oranges. A ragged, dirty little girl was weeping over one wheel, trying to help the donkey, who was, alas, smaller and frailer than Platero. And the little donkey was spending himself against the wind, trying vainly at the sobbing cry of the child to pull the cart out of the mire. His efforts were futile, like the efforts of brave children, like the breath of those tired summer breezes which fall fainting among the flowers.

I patted Platero, and as well as I could I hitched him to the cart in front of the wretched little donkey. I encouraged him then with an affectionate command, and Platero, at one tug, pulled cart and beast out of the mud and up the bank.

How the little girl smiled! It was as if the evening sun, setting among the yellow-crystal rain clouds, had kindled a dawn of joy behind her dirty tears.

With tearful gladness she offered me two choice oranges, perfect, heavy, round. I took them gratefully, and I gave one to the weak little donkey, to comfort him; the other to Platero, as a golden reward.

XXXVIII

BREAD

I HAVE told you, Platero, that the soul of our town is wine, have I not? No; the soul of our town is bread. Moguer is like a loaf of wheat bread, white inside like the crumb and golden on the outside like the soft crust.

At noon, when the sun is at its warmest, the town begins to smoke and to smell of pine wood and warm bread. The whole town opens its mouth. It is like a huge mouth that eats a huge loaf of bread. Bread is life. It goes with everything: with the oil, the stew, the cheese, and the grapes, giving its flavor of kisses; with the wine, the soup, the ham, with itself, bread with bread. Also it may be bread alone, like hope, or bread with an illusion. . . .

The bakers' boys come on their trotting horses and stop before each closed door. They clap their hands and call out:

"Bread! Bread!"

Baskets are held up by bare arms; one hears the thud of the quarter-loaves as they fall against the buns, the large loaves falling against the rolls. . . .

62

And poor children immediately ring the bell at iron gratings or knock at heavy doors and cry, sending plaintive echoes down the corridors:

"A little bit of bread, please!"

XXXIX

AGLAIA

How very handsome you are today, Platero. Come here.
What a fine bath Macaria has given you this morning. All
the white and all the black in you shines and stands out like
day and like night after rain. How handsome you look, Platero!

Platero, somewhat abashed by his appearance, comes to
me slowly, still wet from his bath, so clean he is like a naked
girl. His face has become clear, like a dawn, and in it his
great eyes sparkle brightly, as if the youngest of the Graces
had lent them ardor and brilliance.

I tell him so, and, in sudden fraternal enthusiasm, I take
his head in my arms, press it in affectionate embrace, tickle
him. . . . He, with lowered eyes, shies mildly but does not
leave me, or frees himself in a brief run, to stop abruptly
and wait, like a playful dog.

How handsome you are, my boy, I repeat.

And Platero, like a poor child wearing a new dress, runs
about timidly, talking to me, looking at me in his flight,
showing his joy in the movement of his ears, and stops, pretending to eat some red bellflowers at the door of the stable.

Aglaia, the giver of kindness and of beauty, leaning against the pear tree that displays its triple crown of leaves, pears, and sparrows, looks on smilingly, almost invisible in the transparency of the morning sun.

X L

THE CORONA PINE

WHEREVER I stop, Platero, it seems to me that I stop under the Corona pine. Whatever I reach—city, love, glory—it seems to me that I have reached its green plenitude outspread under the great cloud-flecked blue sky. It is a round, clear beacon in the difficult seas of my dreams, as it is for the Moguer sailors in the storms at the sand bar; safe haven of my difficult days at the top of its red, sharp slope, which beggars take on their way to Sanlúcar.

How strong I always feel when I rest under its remembered security. It is the only thing that has not, as I grew up, ceased to be great; the one thing that has become greater each time. When they cut off that branch which the gale had broken, it seemed to me they had cut off one of my limbs; and sometimes, when a sudden pain grips me, it seems to me that it hurts the Corona pine.

The word *magnus* becomes it as it does the sea, the sky, in my heart. In its shade, looking up at the clouds, races and races have rested through the centuries, as on the waters, under the sky, and in the yearning of my heart. When, in the imprecision of my thoughts, arbitrary images place

themselves at will, or in those instants in which things are seen as with a second sight and beside that which is, the Corona pine, transfigured in a vague image of eternity, stands before me, more murmurous and more gigantic still in its vagueness, calling me to rest in its peace as the real and eternal ending of my journey through life.

X L I

DARBÓN

DARBÓN, Platero's doctor, is big as the dappled ox, red as a watermelon. He weighs over two hundred pounds. His age, by his own account, is threescore years.

When he speaks, he misses some notes, as old pianos do; at other times, instead of words, air whistles through. And these false cues carry an accompaniment of nods, of ponderative hand-wavings, of senile hesitations, of clearings of the throat and spitting into a handkerchief, which is beyond words. A pleasant concert for just before dinner.

He has neither molar nor incisor left, and he eats almost nothing but bread crumb, which he first softens in his hand. He rolls it into a pellet and—into his red mouth it goes. He holds it there, pushing it around with his tongue, for an hour. Then another pellet, and another. He chews with his gums, and his chin then reaches his aquiline nose.

I say he is big as the dappled ox. At the door by the bench, he hides the house. But he is easily moved, just like a child, at the sight of Platero. And if he sees a flower or a bird, he laughs suddenly, opening his mouth wide, with great, sustained laughter whose speed and duration he cannot control, and which always ends in tears. Then, calm once more, he looks a long time in the direction of the old cemetery:

"My little girl, my poor little girl. . . ."

THE CHILD AND THE WATER

IN THE barren and burning dryness of the big, dusty barnyard, which, no matter how lightly one treads, covers one
with fine white dust up to the eyes, the child is at the fountain, forming with it a frank and smiling group. Although
there is not a single tree there, a word fills your heart on
approaching, a name which the eyes seem to read on the
Prussian-blue sky with letters of light: "Oasis."

Morning is already noonday warm and the harvest fly
shrills from its olive tree in the yard of San Francisco. The
sun beats down on the child's head, but he, absorbed in the
water, does not feel it. Lying on the ground, he holds his
hand under the living stream of water gushing from the
spout, and the water forms in his hand a trembling palace
of coolness and grace, which his black eyes regard enraptured. He talks to himself, sniffs, scratches himself here
and there through his rags with his other hand. The palace,
always the same and constantly renewed, oscillates at
times. Then the child withdraws within himself, constrains
himself, sinks within himself so that not even the beating

of his blood, which distorts the so-sensitive image, may rob the water of the form he has caught in it.

Platero, I do not know whether you understand what I am saying: but that child holds my soul in his hand.

XLIII

FRIENDSHIP

WE UNDERSTAND each other. I let him go at his fancy, and he always takes me where I want to go.

Platero knows that on reaching the Corona pine I like to get close to its trunk and touch it, and to look up at the sky through its enormous, light-filtered top; he knows that the narrow path that leads between grassplots to the Old Fountain delights me; that it is high festival for me to watch the river from the pine hill, which, like a sorceress, brings classic scenes before me. If I go to sleep, unafraid, on his back, my awakening always finds me at one of these friendly spots.

I treat Platero as if he were a child. If the road is rough or a little too hard for him, I get down to make it easy for him. I kiss him; I tease him mercilessly. He knows that I love him and bears me no grudge. He is so like me, so different from the rest, that I have come to believe that he dreams my own dreams.

Platero has given himself to me like a passionate adolescent. He protests at nothing. I know that I am his happiness. He even avoids donkeys and men. . . .

LULLABY

THE charcoal-burner's little daughter, as pretty and dirty as a coin, with eyes of burnished black and full lips that seem about to burst with the red blood behind the grime, is at the cabin door, sitting on a tile, rocking her baby brother to sleep.

The vibrant break of Maytime is everywhere, ardent and clear as an inner sunlight. In the bright peacefulness the boiling of the pot in the open fire is heard, with the lowing of cattle from the pasture and the mirth of the sea wind in the tangled branches of the eucalyptus trees.

Feelingly, sweetly, the charcoal-burner's daughter sings:

> "Sleep, little one, sleep
> To please the good Shepherdess. . . ."

A pause. The wind in the treetops. . . .

> "Sleep, my little one, dream
> While the little mother sings. . . ."

The wind. . . . Platero, who is walking gently among the pines, approaches, little by little. . . . Then he lies down on the hard earth, and, soothed by the monotonous lullaby of the singer, he falls asleep, like a child.

XLV

THE TREE IN THE YARD

THIS tree, Platero, this acacia which I myself planted, green flame that kept growing, spring after spring, and which even now covers us with its abundant hearty foliage lighted by the setting sun, was, while I lived in that house that is now closed, the first source of my poetry. Just the sight of any branch of it, emerald green in April or golden in October, used to cool my brow, like the cool white hand of a muse. How delicate, how pretty, how perfect it was!

Today, Platero, it is mistress of almost the whole yard. How coarse it has become! I do not know whether it remembers me. To me it is not the same tree, but another. All this time that I had forgotten it, as if it did not exist, spring has been molding it, year by year, at its own whim, away from my pleasure, from my desire.

In spite of being a tree, and a tree planted by me, it says nothing to me. Any tree that we touch for the first time fills our heart with sensations, Platero. A tree that we have loved so dearly, that we have known so well, Platero, says nothing when seen again. It is a sad truth; but it is useless to say more. No, I can no longer see my lyre hanging from this fusion of tree and sunset. The graceful branch does not bring song, nor does thought spring forth at the sight of the inner illumination of its canopy. And here, whither I so often fled from life with the dream of harmonious, cool, and· odorous solitude, here I am ill at ease. I am cold, and I wish to leave as I then wished to leave the club, the drugstore, or the theater, Platero.

XLVI

THE CONSUMPTIVE GIRL

SHE was sitting up straight in a poor, mean chair, her face a dead white, like a bruised lily, in the center of the cold, whitewashed room. The doctor had prescribed walking in the country, to take the sun of that chilly May; but the poor child could not go.

"When I get to the bridge," she told me, "you see, sir, just close by, I can't breathe."

The childish voice, thin and broken, would fail her, as a summer breeze sometimes fails.

I offered her Platero for a little ride. Mounted on him, what laughter from her sharp, dead child's face, all black eyes and white teeth.

Women would look out the doorways to watch us pass. Platero walked slowly, as if knowing that he was carrying a fragile lily of fine crystal. The girl, in her spotless habit of the Virgin of Montemayor tied at her waist with scarlet cord, transfigured by fever and hope, looked like an angel passing through the town on her way to the southern sky.

XLVII

BENEDICTION

PLATERO, I said to him, let us wait for the ox wagons. They bring with them the murmur of the distant forest of Doñana, the mystery of the pine grove of Las Ánimas, the freshness of Las Madres and Dos Fresnos, the odor of La Rocina. . . .

I took him, handsome and elegant, to please the girls along Fuente Street, in the low, whitewashed eaves of which the hesitating evening sun was dying in pale rosy ribbons. Then we placed ourselves beside the hedge of Los Hornos, from which the whole road of Los Llanos is visible.

The ox wagons were already coming uphill. The soft sprinkling of holy water was falling on the green vineyards like a passing blue-gray cloud. But the people did not even raise their eyes to see it.

The gay bridal couples passed first, on donkeys, mules, and horses decorated in the Moorish manner and with braided manes: the bridegrooms gaily boisterous, the brides modestly grave. The rich, vivid multitude went and came, caught up with each other in senseless bedlam. Then came the carriage of the drunkards, noisy, violent, and disorderly. Behind them, the oxcarts, like beds draped in white, with dark-eyed, firm-fleshed, fresh-cheeked girls sitting under the canopy playing tambourines and screeching *sevillanas*. More horses, more donkeys, and the bald, lean, red foreman, his wide-brimmed hat hanging down his back and his golden wand resting on his stirrup:

"Long live the Virgin of the Benediction! . . ."

At last, gently drawn by two huge, docile oxen who looked like bishops, their foreheads ornamented with vivid colors and small mirrors in which the damp sun glittered, the standard of the Sinless One, all amethyst and silver, nodding with the uneven gait of the oxen, in its white carriage covered with flowers like a well-laden garden of withering blooms.

In the distance and smothered in the pealing of bells and the noise of fireworks and the hard clash of horses' hooves on the stones, the music was becoming audible.

Platero then bent his forelegs, and, mild and humble and confident, he knelt—a trick of his—as a woman might.

XLVIII

RONSARD

HAVING freed Platero from his halter and left him grazing among the chaste daisies of the little meadow, I have thrown myself under the pine tree, have taken a small volume from my Moorish saddlebags, and, opening it at a marked place, I have begun to read aloud:

"Comme on voit sur la branche au mois de mai la rose
En sa belle jeunesse, en sa première fleur,
Rendre le ciel jaloux de . . ."

Above, on the topmost boughs, a brief bird leaps and chirps, while the sun turns him and the whole soughing treetop into gold. Joined to its fluttering and to its twittering comes the sound of the breaking of seeds which the bird is eating.

". . . jaloux de sa vive couleur . . ."

A huge warm thing advances suddenly, like a living prow, on my shoulder. It is Platero, who, no doubt attracted by the lyre of Orpheus, comes to read with me. We read:

". . . vive couleur,
Quand l'aube de ses pleurs au point du jour l'a . . ."

But the bird, whose metabolism must be rapid, blots out the word with a discord. How Ronsard, forgetting for a moment his sonnet, "Quand en songeant ma follâtre j'acolle, . . ." must have laughed in hell.

PEEP SHOW

SUDDENLY, monotonously, the silence of the street is broken by the harsh rolling of a little drum. Then a cracked voice spasmodically sends forth a long, trembling cry. The sound of running feet is heard down the street. Children cry:

"The peep-show man! The peep-show man!"

In the corner a small green box with four little red flags waits invitingly on its stand. The old man beats and beats his drum. A group of penniless children, hands in pockets or clasped behind, silently surround the little box. Presently another one arrives running, his penny clutched tightly in the palm of his hand. He steps forward, looks eagerly into the disc.

"Now ... General Prim ... on his white horse! ..." says the old peep-show man wearily, and he beats his drum.

"The port of Barcelona! ..." And more rolling.

Other children arrive with pennies ready and hand them at once to the old fellow, regarding him with rapt attention, impatient to buy his make-believe.

"Now ... the castle of Havana! ..." And the drum rolls.

Platero, who has gone with a neighbor's little girl and

her dog to see the show, puts his head playfully between the children's heads. The old man, with sudden good humor, says to him:

"Where is your penny?"

And the empty-handed children laugh cheerlessly, looking at the peep-show man with humble, flattering solicitude.

L

WAYSIDE FLOWER

How pure, Platero, and how lovely, this wayside blossom. All the bustle and confusion pass beside it: the bulls, the goats, the stallions, men—and it, so delicate and so weak, remains erect, mauve and fine in its place, uncontaminated by any impurity.

Each day when starting up the slope we take the cross-path, you have seen it on its green stand. Now there is a bird by its side that flies away—why?—when we approach; now it is full, like a tiny chalice, of the clear water of a summer cloud; now it consents to the foray of a bee or the voluble adornment of a butterfly.

This flower will live brief days, Platero, although its memory may be eternal. Its life will be like a day of your spring, or like a spring in my life. . . . What would I not give autumn, Platero, in exchange for this divine flower, that it might be, day by day, the simple and endless example of our life?

L I

LORD

I DO not know, Platero, whether you can see a photograph. I have shown photographs to some countryfolk, and they could see nothing in them. Well, this is Lord, Platero, the little fox terrier I have talked to you about sometimes. Look at him. He is—do you see him?—on one of the cushions in the marble terrace, taking the winter sun among the geranium pots.

Poor Lord! He came from Seville when I was there painting. He was white, almost colorless in so much light, full like a woman's thigh, round and impetuous like the water at the mouth of a waterspout. Here and there he had a few spots scattered about like black butterflies. His bright eyes were two brief immensities of noble sentiments. He had a touch of craziness. At times, for no reason, he would whirl madly among the white lilies in the marble terrace, which in May adorn everything, looking red, blue, yellow from the sun-pierced colored crystals of the skylight, like the pigeons that Don Camilo paints. At other times he would climb on the roof and create a chirping hubbub in the nests of the martins. Macaria would soap him thoroughly every morning, and he was always as radiant as the crenelated roof against the blue sky, Platero.

When my father died, Lord spent the whole night keeping watch by his coffin. Once when my mother was ill, he lay at the foot of her bed and spent a month there, barely eating and drinking. . . . Some people came to the house one day to tell us that a rabid dog had bitten him. We had to take him to the castle warehouse and tie him there to the orange tree, away from people.

The look that he cast behind along the little alley when they were taking him away continues to pierce my heart as it did then, Platero, like the light of a dead star that still lives, transcending its nothingness with the exalted intensity of its grief. . . . Every time a physical suffering wounds my heart, there rises before me, long as the path from life to eternity—that is, from the brook to the Corona pine—the look that Lord left in it forever, like a tortured footprint.

84

L I I

THE WELL

THE well! . . . Platero, what a deep word, how green and black, how cool, how sonorous! It is as if the word itself, turning, boring, had drilled into the earth to reach the cold water.

Look: the fig tree adorns and destroys the curb. Within, at hand's reach, a blue, sharp-smelling flower has found its way between the mossy bricks. Farther down, a swallow has her nest. Then, below, in motionless shadow, is an emerald palace, and a lake, which, when one flings a rock at its stillness, is angered, and groans. Finally, the sky.

(Night enters in; the silver moon is in the depth, adorned with stars. Silence. Along the road life has fled. The soul escapes to the depths through the well. One can see beyond it the other side of the twilight. And it seems as though the giant of night, master of all the secrets of the world, were about to spring from the mouth of the well. Oh, quiet and magic labyrinth, somber, fragrant spot, irresistible, enchanted scene.)

Platero, if some day I throw myself into the well, it will not be for death's sake, believe me, but only the more quickly to attain the stars.

Platero brays, thirsty and eager. From the well a frightened, disheveled swallow wings silently.

L I I I

PEACHES

ALONG the Sal alley, violet-colored with lime and sun and blue sky, which twists its brief narrowness as far as the tower that marks its end, black and worn on this southern side by the constant beating of the sea wind, slowly come child and donkey. The child, a dwarfish, stunted little man, shorter than his drooping broad-brimmed hat, dips into his fantastic mountain heart for ballads and popular songs:

> ". . . con grandej fatiguiiiyaaa
> yo je lo pedíaaa . . ."
> (". . . with great desire
> I asked it of her . . .")

Turned loose, the donkey, slightly tired by the small load of peaches, nibbles the thin, dirty grass in the alley. Now and then the youngster, as if turning for a moment to the real street, stops still, spreads out his naked, dusty legs, presses himself down upon the earth, as if to draw strength from it, and, aiding his voice with his hand, sings harshly, with a voice that goes childish on the *e:*
"Pea——ches!"

Then, as though he did not care a straw for making a sale—as Father Díaz used to say—he goes back to his absorbed gypsy humming:

> ". . . yo a ti no te cuurpooo,
> ni te curparíaaa . . ."
>
> (". . . I am not blaming you,
> Nor would I . . .")

And he beat on the stones without knowing it.

There is a smell of warm bread and of burning pine. A late breeze lightly stirs the small street. The big bell suddenly strikes three with the grace notes of the small bell. Then a merry peal, harbinger of festivity, drowns in its torrent of sound the bugle and bells of the station coach, which, on its way uptown, cleaves the silence that has fallen asleep. And the wind brings to the roofs an illusory sea, illusory in its odorous, moving, and refulgent transparency, an empty sea as well, bored with its even waves in its solitary splendor.

The child returns to his stance, to his awakening, and to his cry:

"Pea——ches!"

Platero does not want to move. He looks and looks at the child and sniffs and butts the donkey. And both grays understand each other in an indefinable twin movement of heads, which brings to mind for a moment that of white bears. . . .

"All right, Platero; I will tell the boy to give me his donkey, and you can go with him and be a vendor of peaches . . . there!"

L I V

THE KICK

WE WERE going to the farm to the Montemayor cattle-branding. The paved courtyard, shadow-cooled beneath the blue immensity of the afternoon sky, vibrated sonorously with the neighing of the powerful horses, the fresh laughter of women, the sharp, restless barking of dogs. In a corner, Platero was becoming impatient.

"But, child," I said to him, "you cannot go with us; you are too small."

He became so wild that I told Tonto to get on him and take him with us.

What a gay ride along the clear countryside! The smiling marshes were girdled with gold, with the sun in their broken mirrors multiplying the windmills. In the midst of the hard, round hoofbeats of the horses, Platero's thin, sharp trot could be heard, quickened against time lest he be left alone in the road. Suddenly there was a sound as of the report of a gun. Platero had brushed lightly with his mouth the rump of a fine stallion, and the latter had replied with a rapid kick. No one paid any attention, but I saw that one of Platero's forefeet was bleeding. I dismounted, and with a horsehair and a thorn I bound the broken vein. Then I told Tonto to take him home.

Slowly and sadly, the two turned back along the dry bed of the creek that leads to the town, turning their heads longingly at the brilliant fleetness of our cavalcade.

When, returned from the farm, I went to see Platero, I found him dejected and sorrowful.

"Do you not see," I whispered, "that you cannot go anywhere with grown men?"

ASSOGRAPHY

I READ in a dictionary: *Assography: n.: used, ironically, of the description of an ass.*

Poor donkey! So good, so noble and knowing as you are! Ironically. . . . Why? Don't you even deserve a serious description, you whose real description would be as a story of springtime? Why, a man who is kind should be called an ass. And a bad donkey should be called a man. Ironically. . . . Of you, so intellectual, friend of old men and children, of brook and butterfly, of the sun, of the dog, of the flower and the moon; patient, thoughtful, melancholy, and loving, Marcus Aurelius of the meadows.

Platero, who no doubt understands, looks at me out of his great shining eyes of a soft hardness in which the sun is gleaming small and sparkling in a brief convex sky of blackish green. Oh, if his huge, hairy, idyllic head could know that I do him justice, that I know better than those men who write dictionaries, that I am almost as good as he!

And I have written in the margin of the book: *Assography: n.: should be used, ironically, of course, of the description of the imbecile who writes dictionaries.*

LVI

CORPUS CHRISTI

As WE come into town by Fuente Street on our return from the orchard, the bells, which we had already heard three times from Arroyos, touch the white town with the bronze peals that seem to hover tangibly above it. Their chiming soars amid the fiery and noisy mounting of the firecrackers, black in the daylight, and the shrill metallic raucousness of the music.

The recently whitewashed street with its red-ocher border sports the greenness of poplars and willows. The windows display bedspreads of garnet damask, yellow percale, light-blue satin, and, where there is mourning, candid white with black bands. By the last houses, at the turn of the Porche, the Cross of the Mirrors appears, gathering to itself the rays of the setting sun as well as the light of the red candles that drip rose wax everywhere. Slowly the procession goes by. The crimson banner, and San Roque, patron saint of bakers, laden with tender rolls; the sea-green banner, and San Telmo, patron saint of sailors, with his silver ship in his hands; the yellow banner, and San Isidro, patron saint of farmers, with his little yoke of oxen; and

93

more flags and more colors and more saints; and then Santa Ana, teaching the Virgin as a child; and San José, in gray; and the Immaculate, in blue. . . . At the end, escorted by the Civil Guard, the Reliquary, its silver openwork adorned with scarlet sprays and emerald grapes, slowly approaches in a blue cloud of incense smoke.

In the dusky light, the Andalusian Latin of the Psalms rises clear. Coming through Río Street, the now rosy sun breaks its low ray on the old gold of the dalmatics and ceremonial vestments. Above, around the scarlet tower, the doves weave their garland of glowing white on the smooth opal of the quiet June hour.

In that space of silence, Platero brays. And his gentleness becomes associated with the bell, with the rocket, with the Latin, and with the music of Modesto, which return then to the clear mystery of the day; and his bray, from haughty, turns sweet; from humble, becomes divine.

LVII

PROMENADE

How pleasantly we go along the deep, honeysuckle-hung roads of summer. I read or sing or recite verses to the sky. Platero nibbles the thin grass on the shady roadside, the dusty blooms of the mallows, the yellow vinegar flowers. He spends more time standing than walking. I let him. . . .

The infinitely blue sky, receiving the arrows of my ecstatic eyes, rises to glorious space above the laden almond trees. The entire ardent and silent countryside is gleaming. In the river a small sail stands still in the windless water. The compact smoke of a fire swells in round black clouds toward the hills.

But our journey is short. It is like a sweet defenseless day in the midst of multiple life. Not the apotheosis of the day, nor the sea to which the river goes; not even the tragedy of the flames.

When in the smell of orange blossoms the gay, cool sound of the well pulley is heard, Platero brays and frisks with delight. What a simple daily pleasure. At the cistern I fill my glass and drink that liquid snow. Platero sinks his mouth in the dark water and sips greedily here and there in the cleanest spots.

LVIII

THE COCKFIGHT

I DO NOT know to what I can compare that indefinable
physical discomfort, Platero. . . . A scarlet and gold sharp-
ness that did not have the enchantment of our country's
flag against the sea or against the blue sky. Yes. Perhaps a
Spanish flag against the blue sky of a bull ring, a half-alien
one, like the railroad stations from Huelva to Seville. The
red and yellow of discomfort, as in Galdos' books, in the
cigar-store posters, in the bad pictures of the war in Africa.
. . . A discomfort such as I have always felt from looking
at fine playing cards with cattlemen's brands in the diamonds, or the chromos on tobacco boxes and raisin boxes,
the wine-bottle labels, the "rewards of merit" of the
Puerto school, the little pictures in chocolate bars. . . .

Why was I there or who took me there? The warm winter noonday seemed to me like a French horn in Modesto's
band. . . . There was a smell of new wine, of belched
sausage, of tobacco. . . . The deputy was there, with the
mayor and Litri, that fat and glossy bullfighter from
Huelva. . . . The fighting pit was small and green; and it

was flanked by congested faces overflowing the wooden enclosure, faces congested like the entrails of slaughtered cattle or hogs, faces where the vulgar heart showed through in eyes bloodshot with the wine, the heat, and the excitement of the carnage. The shouts came from the eyes.
. . . It was warm, and everything—such a small world, that of the cockfight—was closed.

And in the broad ray of sunlight, which clouds of slow blue smoke ceaselessly crossed, drawing upon it as on a sort of turbid glass, the poor English cocks, two monstrous harsh red flowers, were tearing each other, spiking each other's eyes, piercing one another in rhythmic leaps, with man's hate, goring each other completely with their lemoned or poisoned spurs. They made no noise at all, they saw nothing, they were not even there. . . .

But what about me? Why was I there, and so sick? I do not know. From time to time I turned to look with infinite longing through a torn canvas that, trembling in the wind, resembled the sail of a boat, at a healthy orange tree that in the pure sunshine outside scented the air with its load of orange blossoms. . . . How good to be—thought my soul—an orange tree in bloom, to be the fresh wind, the high sun!

. . . And yet I did not leave. . . .

NIGHTFALL

IN THE peaceful subdued retreat of village twilights, how much poetry there is in the divining of the distant, the confused remembrance of the barely known. It is a contagious enchantment which holds the town as if nailed on the cross of a long sad thought.

There is a smell of the full clean grain which heaps its vague mounds under the stars—Oh Solomon!—The laborers hum under their breath in sleepy weariness. Sitting in the doorways, the widows think of their dead who sleep so close by, behind the yards. Children run from one shade to the next, like birds flying from tree to tree.

Perhaps, in the somber light lingering on the white-washed walls of humble houses which the kerosene torches are beginning to redden, vague earthy silhouettes pass—silent, sorrowful—a new beggar, a stranger going toward the plowlands, perhaps a thief—their dark, terrifying appearance contrasting with the gentleness which the slow mauve and mystic twilight places upon things known. The children go in, and in the mystery of the lightless doorways there is talk of men who "extract" the fat of children to heal the King's consumptive daughter.

L X

THE STAMP

THAT one was shaped like a watch, Platero. The little silver box opened and there it was, pressed against the purple ink pad, like a bird in its nest. What a delight when, after holding it for a moment against the fine white and mauve palm of my hand, the stamped words appeared:

FRANCISCO RUIZ

MOGUER.

How I envied that stamp of my school friend in Don Carlos' school! With a small home printing set that I found in the attic in an old desk, I tried to make one with my name. But it did not come out right, and, in particular, it was difficult to get an impression. It was not like the other one which with such ease left here and there, in a book, on the wall, on one's flesh, its legend:

FRANCISCO RUIZ
MOGUER.

One day there came to my house, with Arias the silversmith from Seville, a traveling salesman of desk accessories. What a ravishing array of rulers, compasses, colored inks, and stamps! They were of all shapes and sizes. I broke my savings bank and with a duro I found I ordered a stamp with my name and town. What a long week that was. What heart flutterings when the mail arrived. What a disappointment when the postman's footsteps passed our house in the rain. At last, one night, he brought it. It was a small, complicated gadget, with pencil, pen, initials for sealing wax . . . what not! And when I touched a spring, the stamp appeared, brand new, shining bright.

Was anything left unmarked in my house? What was not mine? If someone borrowed the stamp, "Careful! It will wear out!" What anguish! The following day with what gladsome haste I carried everything to school, everything— books, smock, hat, shoes, hands, marked with the legend:

JUAN RAMÓN JIMÉNEZ
MOGUER.

L X I

THE MOTHER DOG

THE bitch I am telling you about, Platero, is the one belonging to Lobato, the sharpshooter. You know her well, for we have met her many times on the Llanos road. . . . Remember? The gold and white one, like a cloudy sunset in May. She gave birth to four baby dogs, and Salud, the dairy maid, took them to her cabin at Madres because one of her children was very ill and Don Luis had told her to give it baby-dog soup. You know how far it is from Lobato's house to the Madres bridge by the Tablas pass. . . .

Platero, they say that the bitch went about as if crazy all day long, coming and going, searching the roads, climbing fences, sniffing people. . . . At vespers they still saw her near the warden's house at Hornos, standing on some coal sacks, howling dismally toward the sunset.

You know how far it is from Enmedio Street to the Tablas pass. . . . Four times the bitch went and came during the night and each time brought back a little dog in her mouth, Platero. And at daybreak, when Lobato opened his door, the bitch was on the threshold looking sweetly at her master, with all the little dogs in tremulous half-sleep, nursing at her full rosy teats.

L X I I

SHE AND WE

PLATERO, perhaps she was going far away. Where? In the black sunny train that was fleeing northward upon the track above us, seeming to waver in the large white clouds.

I was below, with you, in the yellow waving wheat bespattered with the blood of red hollyhocks which July was already crowning with a little wreath of ashes. And the thin clouds of blue smoke—remember?—rolling vainly toward nothingness, saddened for a moment the sun and the flowers.

Brief blond head, veiled in black. . . . She was like the image of illusion in the fleeting frame of the train window.

Perhaps she thought: "I wonder who that man in mourning is, and that little silver donkey?"

Who could it be, indeed? You and I . . . eh, Platero?

L X I I I

S P A R R O W S

THE morning of Santiago Day is clouded with gray and white, as if set in cotton. Everyone has gone to church. The sparrows and Platero and I have remained in the garden.

Sparrows! Under the round clouds which at times rain a few drops, how they come and go in the climbing vines, how they shrill, how they peck at each other's bills! One lights on a bough, takes flight, and leaves it quivering; another drinks a bit of sky from the little pool on the well curb; another has leapt up to the roof from the olive tree, whose almost-dry flowers the gray day brightens in contrast.

Blessed birds, with no fixed holy days! Free in the monotony of the innate, the real, bells mean nothing to them, unless it be a vague joyousness. Well content, with no fatal obligations, with no Olympus to enrapture nor Avernus to terrify them, with no morality but their own nor any God but the blue, they are my brothers, my sweet brothers.

They travel without money and without luggage; they leave a house when the fancy strikes them; they know where to find a brook; they divine a fern; and they need but open their wings to gain happiness. They know nothing of Mondays or Saturdays; they bathe anywhere, any time; they love nameless love, the universal loved one.

And when people—poor wretched people—go to church on Sundays, locking their doors behind them, they, in a glad example of riteless love, suddenly come, with their fresh and jovial shrilling, to the gardens of the closed houses in which some poet whom they know well, and a tender small donkey—will you let me join our names, Platero?—watch them with fraternal love.

L X I V

FRASCO VÉLEZ

TODAY we must not go out, Platero. I have just read in Escribanos Square the mayor's proclamation:

"Every canine that is found on the streets of the Noble City of Moguer without its corresponding *Sálamo* or muzzle will be shot to death by the policemen under my Authority."

That means, Platero, that there are rabid dogs in the town. Over toward Monturrio, the castle, Trasmuros, ever since last night I have been hearing shots and more shots

from the "municipal flying night guard"—another creation of Frasco Vélez.

Lolilla, the idiot girl, shouts at doors and windows that there are no such rabid dogs, and that our present mayor, just as the former one, Vasco, used to disguise Tonto as a ghost, seeks the solitude that the shots leave him to distill his agave and fig brandies. But suppose it were true, and a mad dog bit you? I do not want to think of it, Platero!

L X V

SUMMER

PLATERO is bleeding a thick purple blood from the bites of the horseflies. The harvest fly saws a pine tree that never falls. On opening my eyes after an immense sleep that lasted an instant, I find the sandy landscape turning white, cold in its ardor, spectral.

The low reed brakes are starred with their great vague blooms, roses of smoke, of gauze, of silken paper, with the four carmine teardrops; and an asphyxiating limelike dust whitens the scrubby pines. An unknown bird, yellow with black patches, mute on a bough, becomes part of the scene.

The wardens of the grove sound their brass horns to frighten away the birds that come in great, heaven-sweeping bands to steal the oranges. . . . When we reach the shade of the big oak tree, I break two watermelons that open their red frostiness in a long, cool, crackling sound. I eat mine slowly, listening to the distant village vesper bells. Platero drinks the sweet heart of his, as if it were water.

L X V I

FOREST FIRE

THE big bell! . . . Three . . . four peals . . . Fire!

We left the dinner table, and, our hearts constricted by the narrowness of the wooden staircase, we mounted to the roof in excited, labored silence.

"It is the Lucena field!" cries Anilla, who was already there, above the stairway, before we came out in the night. . . . Ding, dong! Ding, dong! As we reach outdoors—' what a relief—the bell clears its hard, sonorous peal and hammers at our ears and oppresses our hearts.

"How big, how big. . . . It is a great fire. . . ."

Yes. In the black horizon of pines the distant flame appears motionless in its curtailed limpidity. It is like a black and vermilion enamel, like Piero di Cosimo's "The Chase," in which fire is painted in only pure black, red, and white. At times it shines with greater brilliance; at others the red is almost rose, color of the nascent moon. . . . The August night is high and still, as though the fire were forever a part of it, like an eternal element. . . . A shooting star covers half the sky in its flight and sinks in the blue, above Monjas. . . . I am alone. . . .

The braying of Platero down below brings me back to reality. Everyone has gone down. And in a chill with which the mildness of the night—for it is growing late—touches me, I feel as if there had just passed by me the man who as a child I thought was the one who burned the forests, a sort of Joe the Sly—a Moguerian Oscar Wilde—now somewhat old, dark-skinned and with gray curls, his effeminate roundness dressed in black jacket and trousers of white and maroon plaid, whose pockets bulged with long Gibraltar matches. . . .

LXVII

THE BROOK

THIS brook, Platero, now dry and serving as a road to the horse farm, is in all my yellowed books, at times in its verity beside the caved-in well of its meadow, with its sunpierced buttercups and its drooping wild roses; at other times in allegorical superpositions and changes transported by my feeling to remote scenes, scenes nonexistent, perhaps, or only intuitively suspected.

By its side, Platero, my childish fancy was awakened, smiling like a flower in the sun, when I learned that it itself, the Brook of the Plains, was the same brook that crosses the road to San Antonio beside the little group of singing elms; that walking its dry bed in summer, one came here; that a little cork boat dropped there, at the elms, in winter, would sail down to these pomegranate trees, my refuge from the bulls, under the Angustias bridge.

What enchantment in the fancies of childhood, Platero; I do not know whether you have had them. Everything comes and goes, in a delightful lightning change; everything is seen and not seen, rather like a momentary image in the mind. . . . And one goes about semiblind, seeing as much within as without, at times overturning in the shadow of the soul the load of images of life felt or seen or imagined; or opening the poetry of the illuminated soul to the sun like a flower, placing it on a shore which nevermore is found.

LXVIII

SUNDAY

THE clamorous voice of the bell, now near, now far, resounds in the sky as if the blue were a crystal goblet. And the open country, already a little sickly, seems to gild itself with open notes falling from the joyous chiming.

Everyone, even the watchman, has gone to town to see the procession. Platero and I are alone. What peace! What freedom! What well-being! I turn Platero loose in the meadow, and, under a pine which the birds have not deserted, I fling myself on the ground to read Omar Khayyám.

The silence between two peals, the inner tumult of the September morning, acquire shape and sound. The gold and black wasps flutter round the bunches of muscatel grapes which load the vine; the butterflies, indistinguishable from the flowers, seem to renew themselves in a metamorphosis of color as they fly. The solitude is like a great thought of light.

Now and then Platero stops eating and looks at me. I, now and then, stop reading and look at Platero.

LXIX

THE CRICKET'S SONG

FROM our nocturnal ramblings, Platero and I have become familiar with the song of the cricket.

The first song of the cricket, at dusk, is hesitant, low,

and harsh. It changes tone, learns a little from itself, rises gradually as if seeking the harmony of the place and of the hour. Suddenly, when stars have appeared in the green limpid sky, the song attains the melodious sweetness of a silver bell.

The cool breezes come and go; night flowers open wide; and over the plain hovers a pure divine essence of blue meadows, celestial and terrestrial. And the song of the cricket is exultant, fills the fields like the voice of the shadow. It no longer hesitates, nor does it stop. As proceeding from itself, each note is twin of the other, a fraternity of dark crystals.

Serenely, the hours pass. There is no war in the world, and the laborer sleeps well, seeing the sky in the depth of his slumber. Perhaps love, hid in the climbing vines of the garden wall, knows ecstasy, eyes looking into eyes. The fields send the town messages of tender fragrance in candorous, naked adolescence. And the wheat ripples, green in the moonlight, sighing to the wind of early daybreak. . . . The song of the cricket from its very persistence has been lost. . . .

Here it is. Oh song of the cricket in early morning, when shivering with the cold Platero and I turn homeward by paths white with dew. The red sleepy moon drops. Now the song is tipsy with moonlight, drunk with stars, romantic, mysterious, profuse. It is then that great mournful clouds bordered with a sad bluish mauve slowly bring the day up from the sea. . . .

L X X

BULLFIGHT

I WAGER you do not know, Platero, what those children wanted. To see whether I would let them take you to ask for the key at the bullfight this afternoon. But do not worry. I told them they must not even think of it.

They were crazy with excitement, Platero. The whole town is excited over the bullfight. The band has been playing since daylight in front of the taverns; it is now out of tune; cars and horses go up Nueva Street, down Nueva Street. Back there they are decorating the "Canary," that yellow carriage the children like so well, for the bullfighters' parade. Gardens have been robbed of their flowers for the patronesses. It is a sad night, the young boys staggering down the streets, their wide-brimmed hats askew, their cigars, their shirts, themselves, smelling of horses and of brandy. . . .

At two o'clock, Platero, in that instant of sunny solitude, in that empty moment of the day, while bullfighters and patronesses are dressing up, you and I will leave by the side door and go along the lane to the country, as we did last year.

How beautiful the country is on these holidays when everyone forsakes it! The vineyards are deserted, and the orchards; one scarcely sees even an old man bent over a sour vine or stooped silently above a clear pool. In the distance, over the town, rises the full-throated clamor, the clapping of hands, the music from the bullfight, lost as one wanders on serenely to the sea. And the soul, Platero, feels itself complete master of the great body of Nature which, when respected, yields to him who deserves it the spectacle of her resplendent and eternal beauty.

L X X I

STORM

FEAR. Held breath. Cold sweat. The terrible low sky strangles the daybreak. (And nowhere to escape.) Silence. Love stops. Guilt trembles. Remorse closes its eyes. More silence.

Thunder, dull, reverberating, interminable, like a yawn that does not quite end, like an enormous cargo of rocks falling from the zenith on the town, overruns again and again the deserted morning. (And nowhere to flee.) Everything that is weak—flowers, birds—disappears from life.

Terror peeps timidly out the half-open window to behold God tragically showing Himself in flashes of light. Far in the east, between tatters of clouds, sad mauve and rose clouds, dirty, cold clouds, are unable to vanquish the blackness. The six o'clock stagecoach—it might be four o'clock —is heard at the corner in the downpour, the coachman singing to give himself courage. Then an empty farm wagon hurries along.

The Angelus. A harsh, desolate Angelus sobs through the thunder. The last Angelus in the world? And one might wish that it would stop quickly, or else go on ringing, ringing, to drown the storm. And there is walking to and fro, and weeping, and one does not know what one wants. . . . (And nowhere to escape.) Hearts are rigid. Children call. . . .

And what of Platero, so alone in the defenseless stable in the yard?

L X X I I

WINE HARVEST

THIS year, Platero, few donkeys have come with the grape harvest. It is in vain that the placards announce in large letters: six reals. Where are the donkeys from Lucena, Almonte, Palos, loaded with black liquid gold dripping from their sides: those long mule trains that had to wait for hours for their turn at the vat? Sweet wine would run down the streets, and women and children would fill jars, pots, jugs.

How gay the harvest used to be then, Platero. The Diezmo harvesting! Under the tall pecan tree the singing harvesters would wash kegs with a sonorous heavy rhythm: the men who poured the wine into the kegs would pass, bare-legged, with the jars of sweet wine like ox blood, bright and foaming: and in the background, under the shed, the barrel-makers produced hollow, echoing hammer strokes, surrounded by the clean fragrant sawdust. . . . Mounted on Admiral, I, followed by the affectionate glances of the harvesters, would enter by one door and leave by the other one—the two cheerful doorways opposite each other, the one giving the other its image of life and light.

They would press twenty wine vats day and night. What madness, what excitement, what ardent optimism! This year, Platero, all the windows are nailed up, and there is enough and to spare with the vat in the yard and one or two wine-pressers.

And now, Platero, you must do something. You are not going to be idle all the time.

The other donkeys, with their loads, have been watching the free, idling Platero; and so that they may not think badly of him or bear him a grudge, I take him to the nearby vine, load him with grapes, and bring him very slowly among the others to the vat. Then I take him away when they are not looking.

NOCTURNE

FROM the festive red-illumined town violent nostalgic waltzes rise in the soft wind toward the sky. The tower is visible, solid, livid, mute, and hard, in a wavering purple limbo that is also bluish pale, and away, behind the wineshops of the suburbs, the yellow and sleepy fallen moon sets in solitary weariness on the river.

The countryside is alone with its trees. There is a broken cricket song, the drowsy conversation of hidden waters, a humid softness as if the stars were disintegrating. . . . Platero brays mournfully from the warmth of his stall.

The goat must be awake, for her bell tinkles, tremulously first, then softly. At last it is silent. . . . In the distance, toward Montemayor, another donkey brays. Another one, then, from Vallejuelo. . . . A dog barks.

The night is so clear that the flowers in the garden are visible in their color, as in the daytime. Near the last house on Fuente Street under a red flickering light, a solitary man turns the corner. . . . I? No. I, in the fragrant mobile and golden blue half-shadow made by the moon, the lilacs, and the breeze and the shadow, listen to the profound whisper of my lonely heart.

Moist and yielding, the sphere revolves. . . .

L X X I V

S A R I T O

DURING wine-making time while I was at the brook vineyard one scarlet afternoon, the women told me that a young
Negro was looking for me.

I was on my way to the threshing floor as he came down
the path.

"Sarito!"

It was Sarito, the servant of Rosalina, my Puerto Rican
sweetheart. He had run away from Seville to fight bulls
in the villages, and, hungry and penniless, he had come
from Niebla on foot, his short coat, doubly red, on one
shoulder.

The vintagers looked at him askance, in poorly disguised contempt; the women, rather to please the men
than from personal ill will, avoided him. Earlier, when
passing by the wine press, he had had a fight with a boy,
who had bitten his ear in two.

I smiled at him and chatted affably with him. Sarito, not
daring to touch me, patted Platero, who was there eating
grapes, and fixed on me a look of noble dignity. . . .

L X X V

LAST SIESTA

WHAT a sad soft harmony, that of the yellow and faded evening sunlight, when I awake under the old fig tree that has sheltered my noonday rest.

Odorous with the emanation of the rhododendron, a dry breeze cools my drowsy awakening. The huge leaves of the bland old tree, lightly moving in the breeze, enshroud me or dazzle me. It is as if I were being gently rocked in a cradle from sunlight to shade and from shade to sunlight.

Far away in the deserted village the three-o'clock bells are ringing for vespers, their sound carried in the crystal waves of the air. Hearing them, Platero, who has stolen from me a melon of inner scarlet frost, stands motionless, watching me with his enormous sleepy eyes, across which a sticky green fly is walking.

Looking into his tired eyes, mine weary again. The breeze returns languidly like a butterfly that is trying to fly but whose wings go suddenly inert, wings—wings— my languid eyelids suddenly closing.

L X X V I

FIREWORKS

ON September watch nights we would go to the hill behind the orchard house to enjoy, from the fragrant peacefulness that the pond lilies distilled there, the noise of the festive town. Pioza, the old vineyard watchman, drunk on the threshing floor, played his cornet hour after hour, face to the moon.

Quite late the fireworks came. First there were dull, short explosions; then single skyrockets, which, high above, opened with a sigh and were like a starry eye that might, for a moment, see the countryside in red, purple, blue; and there were others whose splendor fell like a naked maiden bowing low, like a blood-red willow dripping flowers of light. Oh, what flaming peacocks, what aerial masses of clear roses, what fiery pheasants in gardens of stars!

Platero, at each explosion, would shudder, all blue, purple, red, in the sudden illumination of space; and in the wavering brightness that enlarged and shortened his shadow on the hilltop, I could see his big black eyes looking at me in fright.

When, as a climax, the revolving golden castle wreath—the one that bursts in a deep thunderclap, at which women close their eyes and stop their ears—rose to the constellated sky amid the distant clamor of the town, Platero, braying in a crazed manner, would run among the vine stumps toward the tranquil pines in shadow, like a soul pursued by the devil.

L X X V I I

THE ORCHARD

SINCE we have come to the capital, I have wanted Platero to see the orchard. We walk very slowly along the iron grille in the grateful shade of the acacias and banana trees, which are still loaded with fruit. Platero's footsteps resound on the pavement, which is moistly bright from its watering, blue with the reflected sky in places, and in places white with wet fallen flowers exhaling a sweet evanescent delicate aroma.

Through the open spaces of the dripping ivy on the iron grille, what coolness and what an odor rise from the drenched garden. Within, children play. And through that wave of whiteness the little carriage with its little purple flags and green awning goes by shrilly tinkling; the hazel-nut-vendor's boat passes, all adorned in garnet and gold with its long strings of peanuts and its smoking chimney stack; the balloon girl with her gigantic floating bouquet of blue and green and red; the taffy-seller, exhausted under his red box. . . . In the sky, through the mass of verdure already tinged by the sickness of autumn, against which the cypress and the palm stand out, the yellowish moon begins to glow between rosy clouds.

At the gateway, when I am about to enter, the blue man who guards it with his yellow stick and his great silver watch, says to me:

"The donkey may not enter, sir."

"The donkey? What donkey?" I say, looking beyond Platero, having forgotten, naturally, his animal form.

"What donkey could I mean, sir, what donkey could I mean?"

Then, realizing the truth, since Platero "may not enter," being a donkey, I, being a man, refuse to; and I go with him along the grille, patting him and talking with him of other things. . . .

LXXVIII

THE MOON

PLATERO had just drunk two bucketfuls of water with stars by the barn well and was returning to the stable, slow and absent-minded among the sunflowers. Wrapped in the warm fragrance of the heliotropes and lying on the white-washed doorsill, I was waiting for him.

Beyond the roof, the distant field, damp with September dew, slept, sending forth the pungent breath of pines. A huge black cloud, like a gigantic hen laying an egg of gold, laid the moon upon the hill. I said to the moon:

". . . Ma sola
ha questa luna in ciel, che da nessuno
cader fu vista mai se non in sogno."

Platero stared at the moon, and, with a harsh soft sound, he shook one ear. He turned to gaze at me, and shook the other. . . .

L X X I X

PLAY

PLATERO plays with Diana, the beautiful white dog that looks like a crescent moon, with the old gray goat, with the children.

The agile and elegant Diana jumps in front of the donkey, ringing her little bell, and pretends to bite his nose. And Platero, pointing his ears like century-plant spikes, attacks her gently and rolls her on the fragrant grass.

The goat walks by Platero's side, rubbing herself against his legs, nibbling and pulling at the cattails of his load. With a carnation or a daisy in her mouth, she stands before him, strikes at the crown of his head, then leaps back and bleats softly, flirting like a spoiled woman.

With the children Platero is like a toy. With what patience he suffers their pranks. How slowly he goes about, stopping at intervals, playing the simpleton so that they will not fall off his back. How he frightens them at times, starting suddenly at a false trot.

Clear evenings of autumn! When October's pure breeze sharpens the limpid sounds there ascends from the valley, earnest of an idyllic joy, a medley of bleatings, brayings, laughter of children, barking of dogs, tinkling of bells. . . .

L X X X

WILD GEESE

I HAVE gone to give Platero a drink. From the silence of the yard we hear, far above, incessant calls that, in the serene night, pass swiftly among the soft white clouds and silver stars.

Wild geese. They are going inland, fleeing from a sea storm. From time to time, as if we had ascended or they had stooped earthward in their flight, the lightest rustling of their wings is heard, the lightest rubbing of their bills.

Hours and hours the calls will continue to be heard, passing in an endless fleeing.

Platero, now and then, stops drinking and raises his head as I do, like the women of Millet, up to the stars in gentle infinite yearning.

L X X X I

THE LITTLE GIRL

THE little girl was Platero's delight. As soon as he saw her coming toward him among the lilacs in her little white dress and her rice-straw bonnet, calling him in a finicky little voice: "Platero, Plateri—llo!" the little donkey would try to break his rope, and would leap just like a child and bray excitedly.

She in blind confidence would pass once and again under him, kick him softly, and put her hand—a candid lily—in his big rosy mouth lined with big yellow teeth; or, holding his ears, which he placed within her reach, she would call him all the affectionate variations of his name: "Platero! Platerón! Platerillo! Platerete! Platerucho!"

In the long days that the little girl in her crib sailed downriver toward death, no one remembered Platero. She,

in feverish delirium, called him plaintively: "Plateri—llo!"
To the dark, sigh-filled house would come the distant,
doleful call of her friend. Oh, melancholy summer!

What an exquisite day God sent for the funeral! September, rose and gold as today, was ending. In the cemetery how the pealing of the bells echoed in the open sunset, road to paradise! I returned by way of courtyard walls, alone and downcast, entered the house through the garden door, and, fleeing from humankind, I went to the stable and sat down to think, with Platero.

L X X X I I

THE SHEPHERD

ON THE top of the hill which the purple hour is gradually turning dark and terrifying, the little shepherd, black against the green crystal of the sunset sky, plays his pipe under the twinkling light of Venus. Entangled in the flowers, whose fragrance has increased as they become invisible, their essence exalting them to the point of giving them shape in the shadow in which they are lost, the clear sweet bells of the sheep as they scatter a moment before entering the town tinkle in the well-known pass.

"*Señorito,* if that donkey were mine. . . ."

The urchin, darker and more fantastic in the half-lit hour, his eyes gathering in all the light of the moment, looks like one of those little beggars whom the good Sevillian, Bartolomé Esteban, used to paint.

I would give him my donkey. . . . But what would I do without you, Platero?

The moon, climbing above the hermitage of Montemayor, has been spilling itself softly over the meadow where the vague clarities of the day still wander about; and the patterned ground looks like a dream ground, like indescribable lace, primitive and lovely; and the rocks are longer, closer, sadder; and the water weeps in the unseen spring. . . .

And the little shepherd boy, now in the distance, calls still, covetously:

"Oh, if that donkey were mine. . . ."

LXXXIII

THE CANARY DIES

Look, Platero, the children's canary was dead in his silver cage this morning. It is true that he was very old. In winter, you remember, he was always silent, with his head hidden under his wing. Then, at the beginning of spring, when the sunshine turned the open living room into a garden and the best of the roses of the courtyard bloomed, he too tried to do honor to the new life, and he sang; but his voice was weak and asthmatic, like the voice of a cracked flute.

The eldest of the children used to take care of him, and when he found him lifeless on the floor of his cage, he cried out, sobbing:

"Why did he die? He had everything. He never lacked food nor water nor anything."

No. He did not lack anything, Platero. He died because he died, as Campoamor, that other old songster, would say.

Platero, do you suppose there is a paradise for birds? Do you suppose there is a green garden above the azure sky full of golden rosebushes in bloom with the souls of white, crimson, blue, and yellow birds?

Listen: tonight the children and you and I will take the dead bird down to the garden. The moon is at its full now, and in its pale silver light the poor songster, in Blanca's white hand, will look like the withered petal of a yellow lily. And we will bury him under the big rosebush.

In the spring, Platero, we shall see the bird come out of the heart of a white rose. The fragrant air will turn sweeter with music, and we shall hear in the April sunshine a magic fluttering of invisible wings and a sweet symphony of clear golden trills.

L X X X I V

THE HILL

HAVE you ever seen me, Platero, romantic and classic at
the same time, lying on the hilltop?

Bulls, dogs, crows pass, and I do not move: I do not
even look. Night comes, and I leave only when the dark
takes me. I do not know when first I saw myself there, and
I even doubt if I have ever been there. You know what hill
I mean: that red hill that rises like a torso above the old
Cobano vineyard.

Atop it I have read all I have read, and there I have
thought all my thoughts. In all museums I have seen this
picture of me painted by myself: I, in black, stretched on
the sand, my back to me. I mean, to you, or to him who

might be looking, my thought free between me and the west.

Someone calls me, to eat or to sleep, from the Piña house. I believe I go, but I do not know whether I remain on top of the hill. I am sure, Platero, that now I am not here with you, nor ever wherever I may be, not even in the grave when I am dead; but on the red hill that is classical and romantic at the same time, watching, book in hand, the sun set on the river. . . .

LXXXV

AUTUMN

PLATERO, the sun begins to be reluctant to leave his bed, and the farmers get up earlier than he does. It is true that he is naked, and the weather is cold.

How hard the north wind blows! Look, on the ground, the little fallen twigs; the wind is so sharp, so straight, that they are all parallel, pointing south.

The plow, like a rude weapon of war, goes to the glad labor of peace, Platero; and on either side of the wide moist path, the yellow trees, sure of future green foliage, light our rapid going vividly, like soft fires of clear gold.

LXXXVI

THE CAPTIVE DOG

THE coming of autumn is to me, Platero, a dog that is tied, barking long and clearly in the solitude of a yard, a court, or a garden which begins to turn cold and sad with the evening. Wherever I am, Platero, I always hear, on these days which turn yellower every day, that chained dog, barking at the setting sun.

His barking is an elegy, as nothing else is to me. These are the moments in which all one's life is in the gold that is leaving, like the heart of a miser in the last golden coin of his vanishing treasure. And the gold barely exists, gathered greedily by the soul and placed everywhere, as children catch the sun in a bit of mirror and carry it to the shadowed walls, joining in one the image of the butterfly and the dry leaf.

The sparrows, the blackbirds begin climbing from bough to bough of the orange tree or the acacia, higher each time, following the sun. The sun turns rose, mauve. Beauty immortalizes the fugitive, lifeless moment, as though forever dead, yet living. And sharp and ardently the dog barks at Beauty, at Beauty dying. . . .

LXXXVI'

THE GREEK TURTLE

MY BROTHER and I found it one day when we came home
by the narrow lane. It was August—that Prussian-blue sky,
almost black, Platero!—and, to keep from getting too
warm, we came that way, which was much nearer. In the
grass by the barn wall, almost like a clod, protected a little
by the shade of Canary—the old familiar yellow tree rot-
ting in the corner—it lay, defenseless. Frightened, we
picked it up with the help of the servant girl and ran panting into the house, crying "A turtle, a turtle!" Then we

washed it, for it was very dirty, and discovered, as from decalcomania, drawings in gold and black. . . .

Don Joaquín de la Oliva, El Pájaro Verde, and others who heard those two told us that it was a Greek turtle. Later, when I studied natural history in the Jesuit school, I found our turtle painted in a book, just like it in every way, with that name; and I saw it embalmed in the large showcase with a little chart that gave it that name also. So, there is no doubt, Platero, that it is a Greek turtle.

Here it has been since then. As children we mistreated it abominably; we would swing it from the trapeze; we would set Lord after it; for days we would keep the poor creature face up. . . . Once Sordito fired a shot at it to show us how hard its shell was. The lead pellets ricocheted and killed a poor white pigeon that was drinking water under the pear tree.

Months and months pass without its being seen. Suddenly, any day, it appears in the coal pile, motionless, as if dead. Another day, in the ditch. At times a nest of addled eggs is a sign of its sojourn in a certain spot; it eats with the chickens, with the pigeons, with the sparrows, and what it likes best is tomatoes. Sometimes in spring it takes possession of the garden, and it is as though it had sprouted a new branch out of its eternal lonely old age; as though it had given birth to itself for another century.

LXXXVIII

OCTOBER AFTERNOON

VACATION days are over, and with the first yellow leaves the children have returned to school. Solitude. The heart of the house, also, with the fallen leaves, seems empty. Distant cries and faraway laughter are heard only in fancy.

Evening falls apace, slowly, on the flowering rosebushes. The sunset glow reddens the last late roses, and the garden, lifting its flame of fragrance to the flame of the dying sun, smells of burnt roses. Silence.

Platero, wearily restless as I, does not know what to do. Hesitantly he comes toward me, considers, wonders, and at last, confidently stepping sturdily and cleanly on the brick floor, he comes with me into the house. . . .

137

LXXXIX

ANTONIA

THE brook was so full that the yellow lilies, hardy gold band of its banks in summer, were drowning in isolated dispersal, bestowing their beauty petal by petal on the swift current.

Where would Antoñilla, in that Sunday dress of hers, be able to cross it? The stones that we tried sank in the mud. The girl walked up along the bank as far as the poplar hedge to see whether she could cross there. She could not. . . . Then in a gallant gesture I offered her Platero.

As I addressed her, Antoñilla blushed all over, her blushes burning the freckles that modestly framed her gray eyes. Then suddenly she burst into laughter and leaned against a tree. . . . Finally she made up her mind. She threw her pink woolen shawl on the grass, took a running start, and, nimble as a greyhound, landed on Platero, letting her legs hang on each side, hard legs whose unsuspected ripeness was encircled by the red and white stripes of her coarse stockings.

Platero pondered a moment, and, in a sure leap, he

reached the opposite bank. Then, as Antoñilla, between whose bashfulness and me the brook now lay, spurred him with her heels, he went trotting across the plain, accompanied by the gold and silver laughter of the jolting, dark-skinned girl.

There was a fragrance of lilies, of rain, of love. Like a crown of thorny roses, the line that Shakespeare gave Cleopatra to speak rounded out my thought:

"O happy horse, to bear the weight of Antony!"

"Platero!" I called out discordantly, feeling outraged and angry. . . .

X C

THE FORGOTTEN GRAPE CLUSTER

AFTER the long October rains, in the golden blueness of the first clear day, we went in a body to the vineyards. Platero carried the lunch and the girls' hats on one side of his little pannier and on the other, to balance the weight, Blanca, soft and white and pink, like a peach blossom.

What charm in the rain-washed countryside! The brooks were full to the brim, the fields carefully furrowed, and on the roadside poplars which still flaunted a few yellow leaves, birds in black contrast.

Suddenly the girls, one after the other, rushed forward crying:

"A cluster, a cluster!"

In the old vine whose long tangled branches still showed some blackened and some reddened dry leaves, the burning sun shone on a clear amber bunch of grapes, brilliant and inviting like a woman in her autumn. Everybody wanted it. Victoria, who reached it first and plucked it, defended it royally. Then I asked it of her, and she, with that soft docility which a child turning into a woman shows to a man, held it to me willingly.

The cluster held five large grapes. I gave one to Victoria, one to Blanca, one to Lola, one to Pepa, and the last one, amid unanimous laughter and applause, to Platero, who quickly caught it between his huge teeth.

XCI

ADMIRAL

YOU did not know him. He was taken away before you came. From him I learned nobleness. As you see, the plaque bearing his name is still above the stall that was his, and his saddle, bridle, and halter are there.

What a delight when he entered the yard for the first time, Platero. He came from the dunes, and he brought me a wonderful store of strength, life, and gaiety. How pretty he was! Very early every morning I would ride him toward the beach and gallop by the marshes, rousing flocks of jackdaws that were marauding the closed mills. Then we would turn into the highway, and he would enter Nueva Street at a firm, short trot.

One winter afternoon Monsieur Dupont, from the San Juan warehouses, came to my house, his whip in his hand. He left some bank notes on the lamp table of the little living room and went to the courtyard with Lauro. Later, at nightfall, I saw through the window, as in a dream, Monsieur Dupont going up Nueva Street in the rain, his *charret* drawn by Admiral.

I cannot say for how many days I was brokenhearted. The doctor had to be called, and I was given bromide and ether and what not, until time, which fades everything, took him out of my mind, as it took Lord, and the small girl, too, Platero.

Yes, Platero. What good friends you and Admiral would have been.

X C I I

VIGNETTE

PLATERO, over the damp soft parallel furrows of the recently plowed dark ground in which there already shows a light cover of green of the sprouting seeds, the sun, whose race is so brief now, showers, on setting, long shreds of sensitive gold. Chilled birds fly to the Moro in large, high-flying bands. The lightest gust of wind bares entire branches of their last yellow leaves.

The season invites meditation, Platero. Now we shall have another friend: the new book, well chosen and noble. And before the open book, the countryside will open itself to us, propitious in its nakedness to infinite and sustained solitary thought.

Look, Platero, at this tree which not a month ago sheltered our noonday slumber with green murmurousness. Alone and small and stark it is limned with a single blackbird among its few remaining leaves against the sad yellow vehemence of the swift sunset.

XCIII

FISH SCALE

FROM Aceña Street, Platero, Moguer is a different town. That is where the seamen's district begins. People there talk differently, with free and vivid figures of speech. The men dress better; they wear heavy watch chains and smoke good cigars and long pipes. What a difference between a sober, spare, and simple man from Carretería—Raposo, for example—and a cheerful, ruddy-faced, dark-haired one, Picón—you know him—from Ribera Street.

Granadilla, the daughter of San Francisco's sexton, is from Coral Street. When she comes to our house she leaves the kitchen vibrating with her vivid chatter. The maids, one from Friseta, one from Monturrio, another from Hornos, listen openmouthed. She tells of Cádiz, of Tarifa, and of the Island; she talks of smuggled tobacco, of dress goods from England, of silk stockings, of silver, of gold. . . . Then she leaves, strutting on her high-heeled shoes, her light and rippling figure tightly wrapped in the fine black crepe shawl. . . .

The maids comment unendingly on her colorful words. I notice Montemayor holding a fish scale to the sun, covering one eye with his other hand. . . . When I ask him what he is doing, he replies that he is looking at the Virgin of the Carmen, who appears, with her open embroidered mantle, under the rainbow, on the scale; the Virgin of the Carmen, patron saint of seamen; that it is true, for Granadilla has told him so. . . .

X C I V

PINITO

THAT one! . . . That one! . . . That one! . . . more stupid
than Pinito—oo! . . ."

I had almost forgotten who Pinito was. Now, Platero, in
this mild autumn sunshine which turns the red sand dunes
into a fire that is more red than warm, that urchin's voice
suddenly raises before me the figure of poor Pinito, walking
up the slope toward us, with a load of blackened twigs on
his back.

He appears in my memory and fades again. I can barely
remember him. I see him for a moment, lean, dark, nimble,
with a trace of beauty in his dirty ugliness; but when I try
to fix his image more definitely, everything leaves me, as
does a dream the morning after, and I no longer know
whether what I was remembering was Pinito. . . . Perhaps
he was running almost naked along Nueva Street on a
rainy morning, urchins running after him throwing rocks;
or in winter twilight he appeared, dejected-looking and
stumbling over the walls of the old cemetery, and passed
the windmill on his way to the rent-free cave—with dead
dogs and heaps of trash nearby—which he shared with
alien beggars.

"More stupid than Pinito—oo. . . . That one! . . ."

What would I not give, Platero, to have spoken only once with Pinito! The poor thing died, according to Macaria, from a drinking spree, in the Colillas' house in the castle ditch a long time ago, when I was still a child, as you are now, Platero. But was he really an idiot? What, oh what, was he really like?

Platero, he is dead, and I do not know what he was like; yet you know that, according to that urchin, son of a woman who doubtless knew him, I am more stupid than Pinito.

X C V

THE RIVER

LOOK, Platero, to what straits greed and favoritism have reduced the river between the mines. There is hardly enough of its reddish water this afternoon to reflect the sunset here and there in its purple and yellow mud; and in its bed little but toy boats can sail. What wretchedness!

Formerly the large boats of the wine merchants—catboats, brigantines, feluccas, *The Wolf, The Young Eloisa, The Saint Gaetan,* which was my father's and which poor Quintero captained, *The Star,* my uncle's, captained by Picón—heaped the sky with the gay confusion of their masts—the mainmasts, children's wonderment!—or they went on to Málaga, to Cádiz, to Gibraltar, low in the water with their cargoes of wine. . . . Among them launches complicated the movement of the water with their grease rings, their saints, and their names painted in green, in blue, in yellow, in vermilion. . . . And fishermen would bring their catch to town: sardines, oysters, eels, soles, crabs. . . . The copper from Ríotinto has poisoned everything. One good thing, though, Platero, with the rich having the nice stomachs they do, the poor can eat the wretched catch of today. . . . But the felucca, the brigantine, the catboat—all are gone.

What poverty! The statue of Christ no longer sees the tidal wave at high tide. There remains only, slender thread of dead man's blood—that of a poor, shrunken, ragged beggar—the anemic stream, color of iron like this red sunset against which *The Star,* dismantled, black and rotten, its keel pointed to the sky, outlines its burned hulk like a fishbone; hulk in which the guards' children play—as longings do in my heart.

THE POMEGRANATE

How beautiful this pomegranate, Platero! Aguedilla sent it to me, chosen from the best in her Monjas brook. No other fruit reminds me, as does this one, of the coolness of the water that nourishes it. It is fresh and sound; it bursts with health. Shall we eat it?

Platero, how pleasant the dry and bitter taste of its difficult rind, hard and obstinate as a root in the ground. Now the first sweetness—dawn turned into a brief ruby—of the seeds attached to the skin. Now, Platero, the tight nucleus, sound, complete, with its fine membranes, the exquisite treasure of edible amethysts, juicy and firm, like the heart of some young queen. How packed it is, Platero! Here, eat. How delicious! With what enjoyment we sink our teeth in the bright abundant red ripeness. Wait a moment, I cannot talk. The sense of taste experiences the same stimulation as does the eye from the labyrinth of restless colors in a kaleidoscope. There, that is all!

I no longer have pomegranate trees, Platero. You never saw the ones in the large warehouse yard on Flores Street. We used to go there in the afternoon. . . . Above the broken yard walls we could see the gardens of the Coral Street houses, each one with its border, and the countryside, and the river. The bugle calls of the guards and the Sierra anvil could be heard. . . . It was the discovery of a new part of town that was not my own, in its full day-to-day poetry. In the sunset light the pomegranate trees near the well glowed like rich treasures in the dappled shade of the fig tree, teeming with star lizards. . . .

Pomegranate, fruit of Moguer, choice ornament of its escutcheon! Pomegranates open in the scarlet sunset! Pomegranates from the Monjas orchard, from the Peral ravine, from Sabariego, in the deep restful valleys with brooks in which the rosy sky remains reflected, as it does in my thoughts, until night is well advanced.

XCVII

THE OLD CEMETERY

I WANTED you to come here with me, Platero; that is why I slipped you in among the bricklayer's donkeys, without your being seen by the gravedigger. Now we are in the silence. . . . Go on. . . .

Look, this is the San José court. That green and shady corner, with the broken-down iron railing, is the priests' burying ground. . . . That small, whitewashed section in the west that merges with the vibrant three-o'clock sun is the children's court. . . . Go on. . . . The Admiral. . . . Doña Benita. . . . The paupers' trench, Platero. . . .

How the sparrows come and go in the cypress trees. See how lively they are. That hoopoe that you see there in the salvia bush has its nest in a niche. . . . There are the grave-digger's children. See with what relish they eat their bread and red-butter sandwich. . . . Platero, look at those two white butterflies. . . .

The new court. . . . Wait. . . . Do you hear that? The jingle of bells. . . . It is the three-o'clock coach going down the highway to the station. . . . Those are the Windmill pines. . . .Doña Lutgarda. . . . The Captain. . . . Alfredito Ramos, whom I as a child, with my brother and with Pepe Sáenz and Antonio Rivero, brought here in his little white coffin one spring afternoon. . . . Hush! The Ríotinto train is crossing the bridge. . . . Go on. . . . Poor Carmen, the consumptive; she was so pretty, Platero. . . . Look at that rose in the sunlight. . . . Here is the little girl, that lily-like child who could not keep her black eyes open. . . . And, here, Platero, is my father. . . .

Platero. . . .

XCVIII

LIPIANI

MOVE to one side, Platero, and let the school children pass. It is Thursday, as you know, and they have come to the country. Some days Lipiani takes them to Father Castellano's, others to Angustias, others to La Pila. Today it is evident that Lipiani is in a good humor, for, as you see, he has brought them to the Hermitage.

I have often thought of having Lipiani make an ass out of you—you know what is meant by making a man of a child—but I am afraid you might starve to death. Because poor Lipiani with the pretext of brotherhood with God and let little children come unto me, which he explains in his own way, makes each child share his lunch with him on these afternoon walks, which he repeats often, and so eats thirteen halves himself.

See how happy they all are. The children, like huge badly dressed hearts, red and palpitant, pierced by the ardent force of this gay exuberant October afternoon. Lipiani, mincing his soft mass in the tight suit of cinnamon-brown checks that once was Boria's, smiling under his big graying beard at the thought of the feast under the pine tree. . . . The countryside seems to continue vibrating after his pass-

152

ing like a many-colored metal, like the great church bell which after the vesper chimes still continues—like a huge green bumblebee—humming above the town in the golden tower from which it watches the sea.

X C I X

THE CASTLE

How fair the sky is this late afternoon, Platero, with its metallic autumn light like a wide sword blade of clear gold. I like to come this way because from this aloof hilltop the sunset can be seen so well and no one disturbs us and we disturb no one. . . .

There is only one house, white and blue among the warehouses and the dirty walls bordered with roquette and nettles, and it looks as though no one lived in it. But it is the nocturnal love domain of Colilla and her daughter, those handsome blond women, almost alike, always in black. In this creek is where Pinito died and where he remained two days without anyone's seeing him. Here is where the artillerymen placed the cannon against Don Ignacio, so confident with his contraband of whisky. Besides, the bulls from Angustias enter the town from here, and there are not even children around.

Look at the red decaying vine through the arch of the bridge over the creek, with the brick furnaces and the purple river in the background. Look at the marshes, how deserted. Look how the setting sun, showing itself large and scarlet like a visible god, attracts to itself the ecstasy of everything and sinks in the strip of sea behind Huelva in the absolute silence with which the world renders it homage—that is, Moguer, its countryside, and you and I, Platero.

THE OLD BULL RING

ONCE more, Platero, in a sudden flash immediately gone, I have a vision of the old bull ring that burned down one afternoon . . . of . . . that burned down, I do not know when. . . .

I do not know either what it was like inside. . . . I have a memory of having seen—or was that one of the pictures that came on the chocolate bars that Manolito Flórez used to give me?—some pug dogs, small and gray as though made of solid India rubber, being tossed into the air by a black bull. . . . And a round, absolutely empty space with tall, very green grass. . . . I am sure only of what it was like outside—I mean, above—that is to say, what was not the ring. . . . But there were no people. . . . I was running about in the pine bleachers, going higher up each time around, pretending that I was in a real bull ring, like the ones in the pictures; and in the rainy nightfall that overtook me I received an impression that has remained in my soul forever of a distant landscape of rich dark green in the shadow, that is, in the cold, of the threatening cloud, with the horizon of pine groves outlined against the lone, slight brightness, unbroken and white, far away above the sea. . . .

Nothing more. . . . How long was I there? Who rescued me? When was it? I do not know, and no one has ever told me, Platero. . . . But all of them answer me, when I speak about it:

"Yes; the castle bull ring, which burned down. . . . Bull-fighters really came to Moguer then. . . ."

C I

ECHO

THE scene is so deserted that it seems as though there were always someone there. Returning from the hills the hunters always walk faster here and climb the palisades to be able to look around and away. It is said that during his exploits in these parts, Parrales, the bandit, used to camp here for the night. The red rock is visible against the sunrise, and on it a stray goat is sometimes limned against the yellow moon at dusk. In the meadow a pool which dries only in August reflects bits of yellow, green, and roseate sky, almost blinded by the rocks that urchins have thrown in it from the height at the frogs or to watch the water rise in a noisy whirl.

I stopped Platero at the turn of the road close to the redwood that closes the entrance to the meadow and stands there black with the dry sabers of its branches; and, making a trumpet with my hands, I cried against the rock:

"Platero!"

The rock, its dry response somewhat sweetened by the nearness of the water, said:

"Platero!"

Platero turned with a startled movement, raising his head and seeming to want to defend it, and stood there quivering with the impulse to flee.

"Platero!" I cried again at the rock.

The rock repeated:

"Platero!"

Platero looked at me, looked at the rock, and curling his upper lip, he gave vent to an interminable bray directed at the zenith.

The rock brayed long in muffled response, a bray parallel to his with a more prolonged final note.

Platero brayed again.

The rock brayed once more.

Then Platero, in wild headlong excitement, became as unmanageable as bad weather and began to rear and cavort, tried to break his bridle, to leave me, until I gradually quieted him with low words, until little by little his braying became only his braying in the cactus.

C I I

FRIGHT

It was the children's dinnertime. Dreamily the lamp cast its warm pattern on the snow-white cloth, and the red geraniums and red apples added a rough gaiety to that simple idyl of innocent faces. The little girls were eating like grown women; the boys discussed like grown men. In the background, the young mother, blond and beautiful, nursing the baby at her white breast, watched smilingly. Outside the garden window the clear starry night trembled cold.

Suddenly, Blanca ran like a weak ray of light to her mother's arms. There was an abrupt silence, and then, noisily upsetting their chairs, all the children followed her example in swift hubbub, turning terrified faces to the window.

Foolish Platero! With his big white head, enlarged by the shadow, the glass, and the fright in the children's eyes, pressed against the window pane, he was gazing, quiet and wistful, at the warm bright dining room.

C I I I

THE OLD FOUNTAIN

ALWAYS white above the evergreen pine grove; rose or blue, though white, in the dawn; gold or mauve, though white, at dusk; green or sky-blue, though white, at night; the old fountain, Platero, beside which you have so often seen me standing for so long, holds in itself, like a key or a tomb, all the elegy of the world; that is, the sense of real life.

In it I have seen the Parthenon, the Pyramids, all the cathedrals. Every time a mausoleum, a fountain, a portico has kept me awake with the insistence of its beauty, its image has become confused in my daydreams with the image of the old fountain.

From it I went to all other beauties. From them all I returned to it. So completely is it in its place, such a harmonious simplicity makes it immortal, color and light are so entirely its own, that one might almost take from it, bodily, the complete wealth of life. Böcklin painted it above Greece; Fray Luis translated it; Beethoven brimmed it with happy tears; Michelangelo gave it to Rodin.

This fountain is the cradle and the wedding feast; the
song and the sonnet; reality and gladness; death.

There it is dead tonight, Platero, like marble flesh amid
the murmuring green; dead, yet distilling for my soul the
drink of my eternity.

CIV

THE ROAD

How many leaves have fallen in the night, Platero. It looks
as though the trees have become inverted and have their
tops underground and their roots stretched to the sky in
ardent desire to plant themselves there. Look at that poplar; it looks like Lucía, the circus acrobat, when, her flaming
hair on the carpet, she raises her beautiful slender legs
which the fillet lengthens.

Now, Platero, from the nakedness of the boughs the
birds will see us amid the golden leaves as we used to see
them amid the green in spring. The soft song that the leaves
sang above has turned below into a dragging, dreary
prayer.

Do you see the countryside, Platero, all covered with

dry leaves? When we return this way, next Sunday, not one will be left. I do not know where they die. It must be that the birds, in their love chats last spring, told them the secret of this beautiful hidden dying, which you and I are denied, Platero.

C V

PINE NUTS

THERE she comes, up Nueva Street in the sun, the little pine-nut vendor. She has raw and toasted pine nuts. I am going to buy, for you and for me, a big penny's worth of toasted ones, Platero.

November superimposes winter and summer in golden and blue days. The sun burns the skin, and one's veins become full, round, and blue like leeches. Along the clean, white, peaceful streets goes the linen vendor from La Mancha, his gray bundle on his back; the fancy-goods dealer from Lucena, loaded down with yellow light, ringing a bell that picks up the sunlight with each tinkle. . . . And slowly, close to the whitewashed wall, drawing a long line on it with a bit of coal, the girl from Arena, bent under her rush basket, proclaims in long and plaintive cry: "Toast—ed pine—nuts. . . ."

Sweethearts eat them together in doorways, exchanging choice kernels between flaming smiles. Children on their way to school crack them with a stone on doorsills. . . . I remember that when I was a child we used to go to Mariano's orange grove, in the Arroyos, on winter afternoons. We carried toasted pine nuts tied up in a kitchen cloth, and my greatest delight was to carry the pocketknife with which we cracked them, a mother-of-pearl–handled knife, carved in the shape of a fish, with two matching ruby eyes in which the Eiffel Tower could be seen.

What a good taste toasted pine nuts leave in the mouth, Platero! They give such high spirits, such optimism! With them one feels secure in the sun of the cold season, as though already become an immortal monument, and one walks with a difference, and winter clothing has no weight, and one might even go exploring with León, Platero, or with Manquito, the coach boy.

C V I

THE RUNAWAY BULL

WHEN Platero and I arrive at the orange grove, the ravine is still in shadow, but white with the frost-covered lion's claw. The sun does not yet gild the colorless and resplendent sky, against which the oak-covered hill shows its finest gorse. . . . From time to time a broad and prolonged murmur makes me look up. It is the starlings, returning to the olive groves in long formations, changing pattern in ideal maneuvers.

I clap my hands. . . . Echo answers . . . "Manuel!" No one comes. . . . Suddenly, a rapid clamor, big and round. . . . My heart beats to its full capacity with foreboding. I hide, with Platero, in the old fig tree. . . .

Yes. Here he comes. A red bull passes, master of the morning, snuffing, bellowing, shattering for fun whatever is in his path. He stops a moment on the hill and fills the valley up to the sky with a short and terrible moan. The starlings, unafraid, continue passing against the rosy sky with a soft sound that is muffled by the beating of my heart.

In a cloud of dust which the now rising sun touches with copper, the bull comes down through the spiny amaryllis to the well. He drinks briefly, and then, superb, victorious,

larger than the countryside, he goes uphill, his horns hung
with tattered vine runners, toward the forest, and is lost
to view at last between my eager eyes and the dazzling sunrise, now pure gold.

C V I I

NOVEMBER IDYL

WHEN at dusk Platero returns from the country with his
light load of pine branches for the fire, he almost disappears under the spread-out submissive green. His step
is short, neat, like that of a wire-walking circus girl, delicate, playful. . . . He seems not to walk. His ears upright,
he might be a snail beneath its house.

The green branches that once when erect on their tree
had in them sunlight, titmice, wind, moonlight, ravens—
what a horror, Platero, that these have sat there!—drag,
poor things, to touch the white dust of the dry twilight
paths.

A cool mauve softness is a nimbus over all things. And
in the country road which presages December, the tender
humility of the loaded donkey begins to seem, like the
year that is past, almost divine.

CVIII

THE WHITE MARE

I AM sad, Platero. . . . Look; when I was crossing Flores Street at Portada, in the same spot where lightning killed the twin children, Sordo's white mare was lying dead. Some almost naked little girls were walking around her silently.

Purita, the seamstress, who was passing by, told me that this morning Sordo, tired of feeding the mare, took her to the pit. You know the poor thing was as old and slow-witted as Don Julián. She could neither see nor hear, and she could scarcely walk. . . . About noon the mare was back at her master's porch. Irritated, he took a vine prop and tried to drive her away with it. She would not leave. Then he cut her with the sickle. People gathered, and in the cursing and joking the mare started up the street, limping and stumbling. Children followed with cries and rocks. At last she fell to the ground, and they finished killing her there. Some compassionate feeling fluttered above her: "Let her die in peace!" as if you or I had been there, Platero, but it was like a butterfly in the center of a gale.

When I saw her the stones were still piled beside her,

she as cold as they. One of her eyes was wide open, and, blind in life, now that she was dead seemed as if it could see. The only light left in the dark street was her whiteness, above which the night sky, very high in the cold, was disappearing, covered with the lightest of fleecy, rose-colored clouds. . . .

CIX

CHARIVARI

TRULY, Platero, they looked fine. Doña Camila was dressed in white and pink and, with chart and pointer, was giving a lesson to a little pig. He, Satanás, held an empty wineskin in one hand and with the other was drawing a purse from Doña Camila's pocket. I believe it was Pepe the Sly and Concha, the errand girl, who made up the figures, Concha having taken some old clothes from my house. Leading the procession went Pepito the Mimic, dressed as a priest, riding a black donkey and carrying a banner. Behind him marched all the urchins from Enmedio Street, Fuente Street, the Carretería, from Escribanos Square, from Pedro Tello Alley, beating tin cans, cowbells, kettles, brass mortars, saucepans, pots, in rhythmic harmony along the moonlit streets.

You know that Doña Camila has been widowed three times and that she is sixty years old, and that Satanás, widowed too though only once, has had time to consume the wine of seventy seasons. It would be something to hear his comments tonight, behind the windows of his closed house, as he sees and hears his story and that of his new wife recounted in effigy and song.

The charivari will last three days, Platero. Then each neighbor will begin taking back what is hers from the altar in the Square before which, when its images are lighted, drunken men dance. Then for a few nights the noise of the children will continue. At last only the full moon and the romance will be left. . . .

C X

THE GYPSIES

LOOK at her, Platero. There she comes down the street in the coppery sunshine, straight, erect, shawlless, looking at no one. . . . How well she carries the memory of her beauty, gallant still, like an oak, her red kerchief round her body, over her blue white-dotted skirt with many ruffles. She is on her way to the town hall to ask permission to encamp, as usual, behind the cemetery. You remember the sordid tents of the gypsies, their fires, their gaudy women, their starving donkeys all around.

The donkeys, Platero! The donkeys of the town must

be trembling, hearing the gypsies from their stableyards. I am not uneasy about Platero because to get to his stable the gypsies would have to leap over half the town, and, besides, Rengel, the watchman, likes him and me. But in jest, to frighten him, I say with a voice charged with implications:

"In, Platero, in! Let me close the grating. Someone will get you!"

Platero, sure that the gypsies will not get him, passes at a trot through the iron door, which closes after him with a harsh sound of iron and glass. He leaps from the marble court into the flower garden; like an arrow he speeds into the stableyard, breaking, in his short flight, the blue morning-glory vine.

C X I

THE FLAME

COME closer, Platero, come. You need not stand on cere-
mony here. The master of the house is happy to have you
here, because he is one of yours. Alí, his dog, likes you,
you know. And I, need I say anything, Platero? How cold
it must be in the orange grove. You can hear Raposo: "God
grant that not many oranges may be burnt tonight."

Do you not like the fire, Platero? I believe that not even
a woman's naked body can compare with fire flame. What
flowing hair, what arms, what legs could win in a com-
parison with these flaming nudities? Perhaps Nature has
no better example of herself than fire. The house is closed,
and night is without and alone; and nevertheless, how
much closer than the fields themselves are we to Nature
before this opening into the Plutonic lake. Fire is the uni-
verse indoors. Red and interminable, like the blood from a
wound, it warms and strengthens us with all the memories
of blood.

Platero, how beautiful is fire. Look how Alí, almost
burning himself, watches it with his bright wide-open eyes.
What joy! We are enveloped in golden dances and shadow
dances. The whole house dances, becomes small and then

immense in easy playfulness, like Russian dancers. All shapes issue from the fire in endless enchantment: branches and birds, lion and water, mountain and rose. Look, we ourselves, without knowing it, are dancing on the wall, on the floor, on the ceiling.

What a madness, what an intoxication, what a glory. Even Love is like death here, Platero.

C X I I

CONVALESCENCE

LYING in the dim yellow light of my convalescent's room, comfortable with rugs and tapestries, I hear from the night street, as in a dream bedewed with stars, light-stepping donkeys returning from the country, children playing and shouting.

I can imagine the large dark heads of asses and the fine small heads of children who, amid brayings, sing Christmas carols in crystal and silver voices. I feel the town wrapped in the smoke of roasted chestnuts, in the effluvium from stables, in the emanation of homes at peace. . . .

And my soul overflows, purifying me, as if a torrent of celestial waters supplied it from the hidden rock of my heart. Redeeming nightfall! Intimate hour, cold and warm at the same time, full of infinite revelations!

Up above, the bells peal gaily among the stars. Platero, caught in the prevailing spirit, brays in his stall, which, in this instant of heaven-at-hand, seems far away. . . . In. my weakness I weep, moved to tenderness, and alone, just like Faust. . . .

C X I I I

THE OLD DONKEY

"...In short he is so exhausted
That each step bewilders him. ..."
("The Gray Colt of the Velezes' Castle Warden")
—*Romancero General*

I DO not know how to leave, Platero. How can I leave the
poor thing here, without guide or help?

He must have come out of the pit. I believe he neither
hears nor sees us. You saw him this morning in the same
ravine, under the white clouds, his gaunt mournful wretchedness, which flies covered with living islands, lighted
by the radiant sun, he unaware of the prodigious beauty
of the winter day. He would walk slowly around, as
though lost, limping on all four feet; and he would return
to the same place. All he has done is change sides. This
morning he was facing west, and now he is facing east.

What a shackle old age is, Platero! Here is that poor
friend, free and unable to leave, even with spring coming
toward him. Or is he perhaps dead, like Bécquer, and yet
remains standing? A child could draw his outline fixed
against the twilight sky.

174

You see. . . . I tried to push him, and he will not move.
. . . And he pays no attention to my calls. . . . It is as though
death agony had planted him in the ground.

Platero, tonight he will freeze to death in this high ravine, pierced by the north wind. . . . I do not know how
to leave; I do not know what to do, Platero. . . .

C X I V

DAWN

IN THE slow dawns of winter, when the watchful roosters
discover the first roses of daybreak and gallantly greet
them, Platero, surfeited with sleeping, brays a long, long
bray. How pleasing his distant awakening in the blue light
that filters through my shutters. I, also eager for the day,
think of the sun from my soft bed.

And I think of what might have been the fate of Platero if, instead of falling into my hands, he had fallen into those of one of the charcoal-burners who go before day on hard, frost-covered, solitary roads to rob the forest of its pines; or into those of one of the unkempt gypsies who dye their donkeys and give them arsenic and stick pins in their ears to keep them from drooping.

Platero brays again. I wonder if he knows I am thinking of him? What does it matter? In the tenderness of the dawn the thought of him is as pleasant to me as daybreak. And God be thanked he has a stable as warm and snug as a cradle, as kind as my thoughts.

CXV

SMALL FLOWERS

To my mother

WHEN Mother Teresa died, my mother tells me, she died in a delirium of flowers. I do not know by what association with the colored starlets of a childish dream of mine, Platero—for I was a small child then—I think, whenever I remember her death, that the flowers of her dying delirium were pink, blue, and purple verbenas.

I remember Mother Teresa only through the colored lead glass of the courtyard grating, through which the sun and moon looked blue or scarlet to me, bending obstinately over the blue flower pots or over the white borders. And the image never turns her face to me—for I do not remember how she looked—under the noonday August sun or under the rainstorms of September.

My mother says that in that delirium she called some invisible gardener, Platero. Whoever he was, he must have taken her gently along a path of flowers, of verbenas. By that road she returns to me, in my memory, to me who in my loving understanding keep her to her taste, although wholly outside my heart, as among those fine silks she used to wear, all sprayed over with tiny flowers, sisters also to the fallen heliotropes in the garden and to the starlets of my childhood nights.

C X V I

CHRISTMAS

A FIRE out of doors! . . . It is the afternoon before Christmas, and a dim, feeble sun barely lights the raw, cloudless sky, all gray instead of all blue, with an indefinable yellow-

ness in the west horizon. . . . Suddenly there is a strident crackling of green branches beginning to burn; then the thick smoke, white like ermine; and at last the flame, which cleans out the smoke and fills the air with pure short-lived tongues of fire that seem to be licking the air.

Oh, the flame in the wind! Rosy, yellow, mauve, blue spirits disappear I know not where, piercing the secret, low-hung sky; and they leave an odor of live coals in the cold. December outdoors, warm now! Winter with affection! Christmas Eve of the happy!

The neighboring rockroses thaw. The landscape, seen through the warm air, trembles and becomes pure as if it were molten crystal. And the caretaker's children, who have no crèche, come in their poverty and sadness to stand around the fire and warm their cold-stiffened hands, and into the coals they throw acorns and chestnuts, which burst with a loud report.

And they grow gay after a while and jump over the fire, which the darkness turns red, and they sing:

> ". . . Walk, María,
> walk, José. . . ."

I bring Platero and let them play with him.

C X V I I

RIBERA STREET

HERE in this big house, which is now the civil-guard headquarters, I was born, Platero. How, as a child, I liked this modest balcony, Moorish in Master Garfia's manner, with its colored-glass stars, and how grand it seemed to me! Look through the grating, Platero; the white and lavender-colored lilacs and the little bluebells still bedeck the time-blackened wooden railing at the back of the courtyard, delight of my childhood.

Platero, at this corner of Flores Street, the sailors, in rows like the furrows of an October field, used to stand in their uniforms of various blues. I remember that they seemed gigantic to me; for, between their legs, spread out through force of seagoing habit, I could see, far below, the river with its parallel stripes of water and sand, the former shining bright, the latter dry and yellow; with a slow boat on the edge of the other arm of the river; with the background of violent red spots in the western sky. . . . Later my father moved to Nueva Street, because the sailors were always having knife fights, because every night urchins would break the porch light and the doorbell, and because it was always windy at the corner. . . .

From the bay window the sea can be seen. And I shall never forget the night that all of us children, frightened and trembling, were taken there to watch the English ship that was burning in the sand bar. . . .

CXVIII

RAINY SEASON

GOD is in His crystal palace. I mean that it is raining, Platero. It is raining. The last flowers which autumn has had to leave clinging obstinately to lifeless boughs are covered with diamonds. In each diamond, a sky, a crystal palace, a god. Look at this rose: it has within it another liquid rose, and when shaken, see? the new brilliant flower falls, as if it were the soul of the rose, and the rose is left bruised and sad, like my soul.

Rain must be as gay as sunshine. If you do not think so, look how happy the children run under it, sturdy and rosy and bare-legged. Look how all the sparrows, in sudden noisy gathering, enter the ivy—their schoolhouse, Platero, as your doctor, Darbón, calls it.

It is raining. Today we shall not go to the country. It is a day for contemplation. Look how the gutters of the roof are running over. Look how clean and shining the acacias become, black and a little golden still; how the children's little boat that was yesterday among the weeds sails again in the ditch. Look now, in this instantaneous weak sunlight, how lovely the rainbow that begins at the church and dies in vague iridescence at our side.

CXIX

SHE-ASS'S MILK

PEOPLE walk faster and cough in the silence of the December morning. The wind overturns the ringing to mass from the other side of the town. The seven-o'clock coach goes by, empty. . . . I am reawakened by the vibrating noise of the window bars. Has the blind man again tied his she-ass to the bars as he does every year?

The milkmaids run briskly up and down the street, holding their tin buckets against their stomachs, calling out their white treasure in the cold. This milk, which the blind man draws from the she-ass, is for those suffering from colds.

No doubt the blind man, being blind, does not realize the wretchedness, growing worse by the day, by the hour, of his beast. The whole of her seems to be a blind eye of her master. . . . One afternoon as I was going along the Ánimas ravine with Platero, I came upon the blind man beating the poor ass to right and left as the creature slid across the meadow, almost sitting on the wet grass. Blows fell on the orange tree, the well, the air, less violent than the oaths, which, had they had substance, would have demolished the castle tower. . . . The poor old ass wanted

no more offspring and defended herself from destiny by spilling on the barren earth, like Onán, the gift of some impudent donkey. . . . The blind man, who earns his living-in-darkness selling to the old, for a farthing or for a promise, two fingers of baby asses' nectar, wanted the ass to retain, standing, the fruitful gift, source of his sweet medicine.

And here now, rubbing her misfortune against the window bars, is the she-ass, for another long winter the wretched pharmacy of old smokers, consumptives, and drunkards.

C X X

CLEAR NIGHT

THE crenelated white roofs are etched against the cold starry blue sky. The quiet north wind's caresses are keen-edged.

Everyone believes he is cold and hides in the house and closes it. Platero, you and I shall go very slowly through the cleared solitary town, you warm under your wool robe and my coat, I with my soul.

What an inner force uplifts me as if I were a tower of crude stone capped with intricate silverwork! See how many stars in the sky. There are so many they make me dizzy. The sky might be a world of children saying over to the earth a flaming rosary of ideal love.

Platero, Platero! I would give my whole life and wish you might want to give yours for the purity of this high night of January, so alone and clear and hard.

C X X I

THE WREATH OF PARSLEY

LET us see who gets there first!"

The prize was a picture book which I had received from Vienna the day before.

"Let us see who gets to the violet bed first! One . . . two . . . three . . . go!"

The little girls were off in a gay whirl of white and rose in the sunlight. In the silence that their mute forward rush cleft in the morning, the slow striking of the town's tower clock, the slight humming of a gnat in the pine hill that blue lilies covered, and the murmur of running water in the ditch were heard for an instant. . . . The children had reached the first orange tree when Platero, who had been idling somewhere around, caught the spirit of the game

and joined the lively race. The girls, eager to win, could not stop to protest, nor even to laugh. I called out to them:

"Platero is going to win! Platero is going to win!"

Yes, Platero reached the violet bed before anyone else and remained by it, wallowing in the sand.

The girls came back protesting heatedly, rolling up their stockings, gathering up their hair:

"That wasn't fair! That wasn't fair! No, no, no!"

I told them that Platero had won the race and that it was fair to reward him. That the book, since Platero could

not read, should be used as a prize for some other race
of their own, but that we must give Platero a prize.

They, sure now of the book, leaped and laughed with
joy, faces flushed:

"Yes! Yes! Yes!"

Realizing that Platero had had his reward in his effort,
as I have in my verses, I picked up a few sprigs of parsley
from the housekeeper's parsley bed, made them into a
wreath and placed it on Platero's head, as on a Spartan's.

CXXII

THE WISE MEN

WHAT excitement tonight, Platero, for the children! It
was not possible to put them to bed. At last, sleep over-
came them: one in an armchair, one on the floor near the
fireplace; Blanca in a low chair, Pepe on the window seat,
face toward the door lest the Wise Men should pass. . . .
And now, in this remoteness from life, one senses something like a great sound heart, the vivid and magical sleep
of all.

Before dinner I went up with all of them. What a clamor
up the stairway, so terrifying to them on other nights.

"I am not afraid in the skylight, Pepe, are you?" Thus Blanca, holding tight to my hand.

And we placed everyone's shoes on the balcony, among the citrons. Now, Platero, Montemayor, Aunty, María-Teresa, Lolilla, Perico, you, and I are going to dress up in sheets, bedspreads, and ancient hats. And at twelve, we shall pass in front of the children's window in a procession of disguises and lights, playing brass mortars, trumpets, and the spiral-shaped horn which is in the guest room. You will lead the parade with me, who will be Gaspar and wear a burlap beard, and you will have, as a cover, the flag of Colombia which I brought from the house of my uncle, the former consul. The children, suddenly awakened, with sleep still hanging in shreds over their astonished eyes, will look out through the windowpanes in their nightdresses, shivering and amazed. Afterward we shall continue in their dreams, until day; and tomorrow, when rather late the blue sky will dazzle them through the shutters, they will mount, half-dressed, to the balcony and become masters of all the treasure.

Last year we laughed a great deal. You will see what a fine time we have tonight, Platero, my little camel.

C X X I I I

MONS-URIUM

MONTURRIO today. The little red hills, smaller each day from the digging of sand-dealers, which, seen from the sea, look like gold and were therefore endowed by the Romans with that brilliant and lofty name. The way to the Windmill is shorter through Monturrio than through the cemetery. There are ruins all over, and diggers find bones, coins, and pots in its vineyards.

. . . Columbus does not give me much comfort, Platero. Did he or did he not stop at my house; did he or did he not take holy communion at Santa Clara Church; does this palm or this inn date back to his time or does it not? . . . He was hereabouts no doubt, and you know the two gifts he brought us from America. The ones that I like to feel under me, like a strong root, are the Romans, they who mixed the concrete for the castle which no pick nor blow can ruin, into which it was not possible to drive the white stork weather vane, Platero.

I shall never forget the day when, as a very young child, I learned that name, *Mons-urium*. Suddenly and forever

Monturrio became ennobled for me. My longing for the best—so inadequate in my poor town—found a delectable beguilement. Whom need I envy now? What antiquity, what ruin—cathedral or castle—could long hold my imagination on the sunset of illusion? I suddenly found myself as on an inexhaustible treasure. Moguer, hill of slag of gold, Platero; you may live and die happy.

C X X I V

W I N E

PLATERO, I have told you that the soul of Moguer is bread. No. Moguer is like a pipe of thick clear crystal waiting the whole year through under its round blue sky for its golden wine. When September comes, if the Devil has not spoiled the feast, the cup fills to the brim with wine and overflows like a generous heart.

The whole town then smells of wine, more or less generously, and tinkles like crystal. It is as though the sun gave itself in liquid beauty for our four pence, for the pleasure of finding itself enclosed in the transparent cup of the white town and of gladdening its good blood. Every

house is, in every street, like a bottle in Juanito Miguel's or
the Royalist's wineshop when the dying day touches them
with sunset light.

I am reminded of Turner's "Fountain of Indolence,"
which in its lemon-yellows seems painted with wine. Thus
Moguer, fountain of wine which like blood comes end-
lessly to wash its every wound; source of sad gaiety which
like the April sun rises in springtime every year but falls
each day.

THE FABLE

FROM childhood, Platero, I had as instinctive a horror of fables as I did of the church, the civil guard, bullfighters, and the accordion. The poor beasts by dint of speaking foolishness through the mouths of storytellers, became to me as odious as they did in their evil-smelling glass containers in the department of natural history. Each word they said—I mean that a hoarse, yellowed man made them say—seemed to me as unnatural as a glass eye, a wired wing, a support for falseness. Then when I saw trained animals in the circus at Huelva and Seville, the fable, which with notebooks and prizes had been relegated to the forgetfulness of the abandoned schoolroom, rose again like a disagreeable nightmare of my adolescence.

After I was grown, Platero, a writer of fables, Jean de la Fontaine, whom you have heard me speak about and quote, reconciled me to talking animals; and a verse of his has often seemed to me the real voice of the crow, the dove, or the goat. But I always omitted reading the "moral," that dry appendage, that bit of ashes, that fallen feather of the ending.

Of course, Platero, you are not a donkey in the vulgar sense of the word nor according to the definition in the dictionary of the Spanish Academy. You are a donkey as I know and understand the word. You have your language and not mine; just as I do not know that of the rose, nor the rose that of the nightingale. So, do not be afraid that I shall ever—as you may have thought, looking at my books—do not fear that I shall ever make you the false hero of a miserable fable, combining your sonorous expression with that of the fox or the lark, to deduce later, in italics, the cold vain "moral" of the fable. No, Platero. . . .

C X X V I

CARNIVAL

How handsome Platero is today! It is Carnival Monday and the children are wearing masks and gay costumes. They have arrayed Platero in a Moorish harness, heavily embroidered in red, blue, white, and yellow arabesques.

Rain, sun, and cold. Colored serpentine streams from the balconies and bits of confetti are tossed about in the sharp afternoon wind. The revelers, stiff with cold, try to warm blue hands in the folds of their flowing costumes.

When we arrive at the Square, some women, disguised as inmates of an insane asylum in long white robes, their

loose black hair wreathed with green leaves, take Platero in the center of their boisterous circle and, joining hands, dance gaily around him.

Platero, hesitating, pricks up his ears, raises his head, and, like a scorpion surrounded by fire, tries nervously to escape by every means. But, as he is so small, the crazy women are not afraid of him and continue gyrating around him, singing and laughing. The children make great sport of his captivity, imitating his braying, playfully clapping their hands when he answers them. The whole Square is now a confused concert of brayings, laughter, songs, tambourines, brass mortars. . . .

At last, Platero, in a determined fashion like a man, breaks through the circle and comes to me trotting and quivering, his rich trappings almost lost. Like myself, he wants nothing to do with the carnival. . . . We are not good for that sort of thing.

C X X V I I

LEÓN

PLATERO and I are walking slowly, one on either side of the stone benches of Monjas Square, deserted and bright on this warm February afternoon, the early sunset already falling in mauve diluted with gold on the hospital, when I suddenly sense that someone else is with us. As I turn, I am greeted with the words: "Don Juan." . . . And León lightly claps his hands. . . .

Yes, it is León, already dressed and perfumed for the nightfall concert, in his plaid jacket, his white-stitched patent-leather boots, his unfolded handkerchief of green silk, and, under his arm, the shining cymbals. He claps his hands lightly and tells me that God gives each one his own gift; that if I write for the newspapers, he, with such an ear, is capable of. . . . "You can see, Don Juan, the cymbals, the most difficult instrument. . . . The very only one that is played without sheet music. . . ." If he wanted to tease Modesto, with that ear he has, he would whistle, before the band ever played them, the new pieces. "You can see. . . . Each one has his own gift. . . . You write for the daily papers. . . . I have more strength than Platero. . . . Feel here. . . ."

And he shows me his old hairless head, in the middle of which, like the Castilian plateau, a great callous, like a hard, dry melon, is the clear sign of his difficult profession.

He claps his hands lightly, leaps up, a wink in his pox-marked eyes, walks away, whistling some two-step or other, the new piece of the evening, no doubt. But he comes back after a moment and hands me a card:

LEÓN
DEAN OF THE STRING PLAYERS
OF MOGUER.

CXXVIII

THE WINDMILL

How big it seemed to me then, Platero, this pond, and how tall that rim of red sand! Was it in this pool that those remembered rough pines were reflected, later filling my dreams with their image of beauty? Is this the balcony from which I once saw, suffused in entrancing sun music, the clearest landscape I have ever seen?

Yes, the gypsies are there, and the fear of bulls comes back. There is also, as there always was, a solitary man— the same one? a different one?—a drunken Cain who says senseless things as we pass, staring with his single eye at the road to see if anyone is coming . . . and desisting at once. . . . Neglect is there and mournfulness, but how new the former, how complete the latter!

Before seeing it again, Platero, I thought I had seen this spot, delight of my childhood, in a painting by Courbet and in another one by Böcklin. I have always wanted to paint its splendor, red facing the autumn sunset, repeated with its young pine saplings in the crystal pool that the sand undermines. . . . But in the magic sun of my

childhood, there remains only a memory adorned with a mustard hedge, which persistence does not resist, like a piece of tissue paper beside a brilliant flame.

CXXIX

THE TOWER

No, YOU cannot go up the tower. You are too big. If only it were the Giralda, at Seville!

How I should enjoy having you climb this tower. From the clock balcony you would see the white roofs of the town with their dormer windows of stained glass and their flowerpots painted indigo. Then, from the south balcony, which the great bell broke with its weight as it was being taken up, the court of the castle and the Diezmo, and, at high tide, the sea. Higher up, from the bells, four villages and the train that goes to Seville and the Ríotinto train and the Virgin of the Rock. Then you would have to climb by the ironbar, and there you would touch the feet of Santa Juana, whom lightning struck, and your head, emerging from the turret window amid the sun-gilded blue and white tiles, would be the wonder of the children playing in the church court whence would rise to you the sharp clear noise of their delight.

How many triumphs you must renounce, poor Platero. Your life is as simple as the short road to the old cemetery.

C X X X

THE SAND-DEALER'S DONKEYS

LOOK, Platero, at Quemado's donkeys; slow, drooping, with their pointed red load of wet sand, pierced, as a heart might be, by the green olive rod with which they are beaten. . . .

MADRIGAL

Look, Platero. Like the little circus horse in its course, it has run around the garden three times, white as the one brief wave of a soft sea of light, and has gone over the garden wall again. I imagine it lighting on the wild rose-bush on the other side, and I can almost see it through the wall. Look. Here it is again. In reality there are two butterflies; one white one, itself; and a black one, its shadow.

Platero, there are culminating beauties which other beauties try in vain to conceal. As in your face your eyes are the greatest charm, the star is the charm of night and the rose and the butterfly that of the morning garden.

Platero, look how well it flies. What a delight it must be to it to fly. It must be as for me the delight of verse. All its being is in its flight; from its self to its soul, and nothing else matters in the world—that is, in the garden.

Hush, Platero. . . . Look. What a joy to watch it flying so, pure and stainless.

C X X X I I

DEATH

I FOUND Platero lying on his bed of straw, eyes soft and sad. I went to him, stroked him, talking to him and trying to help him to stand.

The poor fellow quivered, started to rise, one forefoot bent under. . . . He could not get up. Then I straightened his foot on the ground, patted him again tenderly, and called the doctor.

Old Darbón, as soon as he saw him, puckered his toothless mouth and shook his bulbous head like a pendulum.

"No hope?"

I do not know what he answered. . . . That the poor fellow was dying . . . nothing . . . a pain. . . . Some root he had eaten, with the grass. . . .

At noon, Platero was dead. His little cotton-like stomach had swollen like a globe, and his rigid discolored legs were raised to heaven. His curly hair looked now like the moth-eaten tow hair of old dolls that falls off when you touch it.

Through the silent stable, its translucent wings seeming to catch fire every time it passed the ray of light that came in through the little window, fluttered a beautiful three-colored butterfly.

CXXXIII

NOSTALGIA

PLATERO, you see us, do you not?

Is it not true that you see how the water in the garden well laughs peacefully, clear and cold; how in the late afternoon the industrious bees fly around the green rosemary that has turned mauve, rose, and gold in the last streaks of sunlight that sets fire to the distant hill?

Platero, you do see us, do you not?

Is it not true that you can see, climbing up the red slope to the old spring, the little donkeys of the washerwomen, tired, lame, sad in the immense purity that unites the earth and sky in a single crystal splendor?

Platero, you see us, do you not?

Is it not true that you see the children running playfully among the rockroses, whose flowers cluster in their branches like a light swarm of white butterflies spotted with carmine?

Platero, you do see us.

Platero, is it not true that you do see us? Yes, you see me. And I think I hear—yes, yes, I hear, in the cloudless sunset hour, mellowing the whole valley of the vineyards, your tender, plaintive bray.

C X X X I V

THE SAWHORSE

ON THE wooden sawhorse I placed poor Platero's saddle, bridle, and halter and took everything to the big barn, to the corner where the children's forgotten cradles are. The barn is wide, silent, sunny. From it I can see the whole Moguer countryside: the Windmill, red, to the left; in front, covered with pine trees, Montemayor with its white chapel; behind the church, the inaccessible Piña orchard; to the west, the sea, high and shining in the high summer tides.

During vacation time the children play in the barn. They play coach, with interminable teams of overturned chairs; they play theater, with newspapers painted with red ocher; church, school. . . .

At times they mount the soulless sawhorse, and with restless impetuous moving of feet and hands they trot through the meadows of their imagination:

"Get up, Platero! Get up, Platero!"

C X X X V

MELANCHOLY

THIS afternoon I went with the children to Platero's grave, a low mound that lies in the orchard, at the foot of a round, fatherly pine tree. April had adorned the damp earth with large yellow lilies.

Titmice were singing above in the green canopy mottled with the blue zenith, and their light trilling, joyous and fairy-like, drifted away on the golden air of the balmy evening like a limpid dream of new love.

As soon as we arrived, the children stopped shouting. Quiet and sober, their bright eyes following mine, they plied me with anxious questions.

"Friend Platero," I said to the earth, "if, as I believe, you are now in a heavenly meadow and carry angel children on your hairy back, have you forgotten me, perhaps? Tell me, Platero, do you still remember me?"

And, as if answering my question, a white butterfly, soft and smooth as waxen petals, fluttered gently, like a soul, from lily to lily.

CXXXVI

TO PLATERO

in the Heaven of Moguer

DEAR, trotting Platero, my beloved little donkey, who carried my soul so many times—only my soul!—along the deep roadways of cacti and mallows and honeysuckle; for you this book that is of you, now that you can understand it.

It goes to your soul that grazes now in paradise, through the soul of our Moguer landscape, which must also have gone to heaven with yours; it carries on its paper back my soul which, traveling among the flowering briers, on its ascension becomes better, more peaceful, purer each day.

Yes. I know that when at the close of day I come slowly and thoughtfully through the oropéndolas and the orange blossoms across the lonely orange grove to the pine tree that watches over your last sleep, you, Platero, happy in your meadow of eternal roses, will see me stop before the yellow lilies that have sprung from your buried heart.

CXXXVII

CARDBOARD PLATERO

PLATERO, a year ago when there appeared in the world a part of this book that I wrote in memory of you, a friend of yours and mine made me a gift of this toy Platero. Do you see it from where you are? Look: he is half-gray and half-white; his mouth is black and red; his eyes are enormously big and enormously black; he carries little clay saddlebags with six flowerpots filled with silk-paper flowers, pink and white and yellow; he can move his head, and he walks on a blue-painted board that has four crude wheels.

Remembering you, Platero, I have become attached to this little toy donkey. Everyone who enters my study says to him, smiling, "Platero." If anyone does not know about you and asks me what he is, I say, "It is Platero." And so well has the name accustomed me to the feeling that now I myself, even when alone, think he is you, and I caress him with my eyes.

You? How inconstant is the memory of the human heart. This toy Platero seems to me today more Platero than you yourself, Platero.

CXXXVIII

TO PLATERO, *EN SU TIERRA*

FOR one moment, Platero, I come to watch by your side. I have not lived. Nothing has happened. You are alive and I am with you. I come here alone. The boys and the girls are now grown men and women. Ruin has finished its work on us three—you know—and on its desert we stand, holders of the highest riches, those of our own hearts.

My heart! Would that the heart would suffice those two as it does me. Would that they thought as I do. But no; perhaps it is better that they do not think. . . . Thus they will not carry in their minds the sadness of my iniquities, of my cynicisms, of my impertinences.

How gladly, how easily, I tell you these things which none but you is to know. . . . I shall order all my acts so that the present will be all of life and to them will seem but remembrance, so that a calm future will leave them a past no larger than a violet, of like color, tranquil in the shade, and having its gentle fragrance.

You, Platero, are alone in the past. But what do you care about the past, you who live in timelessness, you who hold in your possession, as I do here, the sun of each new dawn, red as the heart of the eternal God?

Moguer, 1916

LIST OF CHAPTERS

215